A SUBTLE ROT

STORIES FROM THE OTHER
SIDE OF THE VEIL

JACKIE RABBIT

Throughout all recorded time and in all cultures, there is one constant belief…that of the unseen. Though religions and customs vary wildly, nearly all hold strongly to the idea that there are worlds beyond our own and events beyond our understanding. Whether it be travelers in the lonesome deserts running afoul of the Djinn or a wayward child wandering into a faery ring and disappearing, all cultures have tales of when those hidden worlds become anything but. It is easy to dismiss the old tales as mere bedtimes stories. Or maybe we assume that what magic there once was in the world is now gone. What if the tales are true though? What if the magic never left? What if all the wonder and terror of the supernatural is right here, waiting in the woods, hiding in dark alleys, standing just behind you, breathing down your neck.

This book is a repository of such stories. Some are works of pure fiction. Some borrow pieces and themes from life, some are mostly or even completely true. I will leave it to you to judge what is what. Enjoy, take care and don't be afraid to yell at ghosts.

TABLE OF CONTENTS

THE OVERPASS

It's going to be okay, Anna told herself as she shivered and stomped down the moonlit verge of the highway. Everything is going to be fine. But where the fuck was she? It was so dark out. Without even a vague glow of civilization in the distance and no signs to be seen, she could not get her bearings.

She couldn't believe that asshole had just left her. She could die out here. She could freeze or get eaten by coyotes! Still kind of worth it, though. The greasy, middle-aged redneck who had picked her up had promised to get her to San Luis Obispo. It wasn't until she was already sitting in the cab of his filthy truck and well away from civilization that he mentioned the price of this ride.

Anna was hard up and was used to doing unpleasant things to survive. Yesterday she had gotten her lunch out of a dumpster! There are limits, though. She had already lost so much; she wasn't ready to give up those last couple threads of dignity. She did count herself lucky that his reaction was to simply kick her out. It could have been worse. It could have been so much worse. Still, walking through the freezing darkness, she wondered if it would have been that bad. Would she be warm and cozy now, instead of cold and terrified?

Just as Anna started to question her decision, she felt the first droplets of rain. Could this night get any worse? Within minutes, she was soaking wet and chilled to the bone. If that creep came back, she decided, she would agree to any terms. She wanted to curl up and die in the dark and the cold. The absolute blackness of the night closed in on her as she began to regret every decision she ever made. Had things really been that bad at home? Was this worth it? Would it be that bad to put up with her mother's drinking and screaming if it meant being warm again?

Just as the tears began mixing with the rain running down her face, she made out a shape ahead. An overpass! She was sure of it. She could shelter there until the sun came up, and she could figure everything else out after that. She climbed the steep hill that led up to the small ledge beneath the overpass.

Anna felt an overwhelming sense of relief as she was finally able to sit down on dry ground and catch her breath. She was surprised by how large the space was once she got up there. It seemed to go back really far. Lacking a flashlight, Anna flicked her lighter on to get a look around. It appeared she wasn't the first to take shelter in this place. It was hard to see any details in the fickle light of her Bic, but she could make out several large, lumpy shapes further along on the ledge.

"Hello?" she croaked out. Nothing. She called out again, louder and with a little more steel in her voice. The persistent patter of the rain was the only response. Had someone just left their gear here? The lighter finally heated up enough to burn her fingers, and she reluctantly let its tiny flame wink out, leaving her again in darkness.

She grabbed her backpack then and let out a little exclamation of joy when she found that it truly was waterproof as advertised and that her spare set of clothes and thin blanket within it were bone-dry. She quickly changed out of her soaking-wet clothes and clumsily laid them out on the concrete ledge. She wrapped herself in the thin blanket and laid her head on her backpack.

Staring out at the rain-soaked highway, she realized then that there hadn't been any cars. None. Was it really that late? She might have been in the middle of nowhere, but this was still a four-lane highway. Shouldn't there have been at least a couple cars passing through? She pressed the little button on the side of her watch, lighting it up, and saw that it was only 10 p.m. The world shouldn't be this quiet, she thought.

Just then, she heard a scraping, shuffling sound coming from the other side of the ledge, where the abandoned bindles were.

"Hello?" she called, voice trembling.

Great, here's the part where I get stabbed by some deranged hobo or eaten by a mountain lion. Fumbling her lighter out of her pocket and flicking its meager flame to life, she squinted into the darkness.

"Who's there?"

. She tried to make her voice sound confident, but despite her best efforts, she knew she still sounded like the terrified little girl that she was. The pounding of her heart nearly drowned out the driving of the wind and rain. The lighter heated up again and burned her thumb, causing her to cry out and drop it.

"Shit!"

It was still silent on the other side of the ledge. Anna forced herself to take some deep breaths and tried to gather herself. Probably a mouse or the wind or my stupid imagination.

Just as she was convincing herself that she probably imagined it, she heard the noise again. This time it was unmistakable. A scratching, dragging, shuffling sound. Like raking leaves on concrete. Then a rasping exhalation. A gurgling hiss. Anna scrambled for her lighter. For a terrifying moment, she couldn't find it, but then she felt the small plastic object in the grit next to her. She clasped the lighter in both hands, raised it up and struck the flint. As her eyes adjusted to the space beyond the flame, she saw a single point of light in the darkness before her. It was the light of the flame reflected in the milky, dead eye of a nightmare come to life.

The eye sat in the ruined face of what was once a dog. Where the other eye should have been was a ragged black hole. It might have once been a shepherd or husky mix. It had pointed ears and thick fur, now matted with blood and gore. Its nose was gone, and in its place were empty sinuses and bone. The torn flesh around its mouth gave it a permanent snarl. The world stopped in that moment. Anna's mind could not process what she was seeing. She completely froze. Her heart might have stopped then and there, and she would not have noticed. Then it spoke.

"Hello, Anna," it said, with a voice like gravel and breaking bones. It was the sound of maggots on a hot day. It was the gurgling of blood down the abattoir drain. It was rot and ruin and bad deaths. In those few syllables, she heard death. Not just hers but that of all the world she knew and understood. "Calm yourself, child. I am not the thing to fear in this night."

. Anna thought again of the strangely empty road.

She was frozen. Her thoughts were sending back an error message. So, she just sat. Stock still, wide-eyed and slack-jawed, Anna watched as this abomination crept closer and heaved its broken body into a sitting position about five feet from her. That's when the smell hit. The pungent stench of death. It was like smelling salts, waking Anna from her daze.

"Please tell me what the actual fuck is going on," Anna said in a desperate but almost peevish tone. "Are you even real?"

"Tonight, is a special night. And you are a special girl. The prophecies have come to pass, and the warnings to your kind have been ignored."

As the creature spoke, its tongue lolled out of its mouth. It made Anna think of the squished, dead snake she had once seen in the road, all black and pink and torn. While Anna had always had the fantasy of being able to speak to animals, this was not at all what she had expected.

"What are you?" she asked.

"I am called Dusk," it rasped. "I am here to guide you so that we can bring the final prophecy to pass."

She heard the words, but she could not process them. It made no sense. But was she passed sense now? The situation had taken a dive into the truly bizarre. Maybe this was a dream. Maybe she was actually dying on the side of the road, her skull broken, and this whole scene was just the last firings of failing synapses. Oddly, that thought had a calming effect on her.

What about the smell, though? Could you hallucinate smell this vividly? She felt the cold, solid, very-real concrete beneath her palm. It's gotta be in my head, she thought. This can't be real.

Dusk cocked his head to the side quizzically. It was such a normal dog gesture and completely out of place in this situation.

Her eyes had begun to adjust to the deep dark under the overpass. Had it really been that dark before?

"Please. Please explain to me what is going on," Anna said, drawing her hand down her face in a gesture of frustrated confusion.

"Gladly. There is much to tell," he said in his gurgling rasp.

Dusk lowered himself into a more-relaxed laying position, and Anna also felt her body relax a bit. Then he told a tale. He spoke of the paradise of nature being destroyed by greedy men. He spoke of the innocent creatures of the earth being tortured and slaughtered. He told of the old gods and their rage. He told her of poisoned water and changing weather patterns, causing fire and flood and famine. He told her of a broken contract made countless generations back. He said that those individuals the gods had charged with stewardship of this world had not only failed but had viciously and intentionally torn it apart. He spoke of an old bloodline—the Steward Bloodline, whose knowledge had been lost through the millennia. The lineage of those humans that had been touched by the Gods. He told her that she was one of only a few remaining. He laid out the plan to set things right. He talked of starting over. He spoke until the sky began to lighten.

Anna listened with rapt attention to the tale that Dusk wove. She didn't even notice that the rain had stopped. She thought once more of the empty road.

Dusk spoke again. "Will you renew your people's pledge and help restore the order? There will be death. There will be pain and fear. But those are merely birthing pains. We must break this world so that it can be reborn.".

Anna's fear had completely gone now. She was starting to understand her responsibility.

"Yes," she said steadily.

As they climbed down from the ledge and walked out onto the empty highway, the orange light of the rising sun revealed silhouettes along the embankments and surrounding hills. Animals stood there, more than she could count, more than what seemed possible. Deer and coyotes and rabbits and mountain lions, standing side by side with domestic cats and dogs and horses. They stood still and backlit. Ominous sentinels. Soldiers standing at attention, rallying for the battle to come.

LAMIA

He watched her sip the coffee. Her graceful hands holding the large mug to perfect lips. The late morning sun shone in her dark hair like a luminous crown. She was a goddess come down to earth sitting there on the coffee shop patio. She came here every day and so he did as well. He wasn't at the coffee shop. No, that would be too close. She might notice him and that was a risk he couldn't take. He was across the street on a park bench. With a coffee of his own in one hand and his phone in the other, he looked like any other citizen. No one knew there was a beast in their midst. His dark glasses allowed him to stare with impunity. His casual, unassuming clothes made him look inconsequential. His haircut made him look like every other generic thirty something white male. Like a tiger's stripes, these things helped the predator fade into the scenery. He casually angled his phone up slightly to take a picture of his coffee shop beauty.

This was all habit for him now. He had practiced and perfected the process over the years. The finding. The coveting and finally the possessing and destroying. She looked so regal.

He couldn't wait to see that pride get stripped away to be replaced by fear and humiliation. He would have fun breaking her, owning her.

The woman finished her coffee, checked her phone, and stood up to leave. It was time for her to do the weekly grocery shopping. He knew her habits now. Over the last couple of months, he had gotten to know every facet of her life. He had passed her in the grocery isle, brushing against her just slightly. He had ridden the bus with her to work and took in the intoxicating scent of her hair as he stood behind her. He knew that she liked comedy and horror movies over romantic themes. He knew that she ate avocados with her eggs. He knew that she carried herself like she was the queen of the world and treated men like they should bow to her. He knew that her two roommates would be out of town for the next few days to go to a music festival and that she would be all alone.

There was much to do in preparation for this evening. Tonight, was the night. It was the perfect situation. He and his quarry would have the house to themselves for at least two days. The great, old Victorian she lived in had a large basement that would be perfect for what he had planned. Twice he had managed to gain access to the house to get a sense of the space and nab a couple souvenirs. The panties he had taken were in his pocket now and he touched them softly. Soon he would touch the rest of her. Soon he would have all of her.

Waiting for a few minutes after she left, he got up as well and walked to his grey nondescript sedan and drove home to prepare. He lived in a simple stucco townhouse in a neighborhood of similarly nondescript dwellings. The lawn was neat and without decoration. He smiled and waved at a neighbor walking by as he pulled into the driveway. Being a friendly neighbor was important. Not too friendly though. Nothing noteworthy. He blended pleasantly into the background. He did everything he could to be pleasantly unworthy of note.

Once inside he went to a hall closet and pulled out a duffel bag along with shopping bags from several different stores. He always made sure never to buy everything at one place. Even going as far as driving to other towns to spread out the shopping. He always paid in cash and wore different outfits. It was all planned and practiced. In the beginning he had been sloppier and more disorganized. He thought back on some of his earlier prizes and had to chuckle at how haphazard and naive he had been. These days his process was nearly perfect. He had also learned patience. No longer was he the over eager impatient impulsive boy of his youth. No, he was focused and calculating. Nothing was left to chance. The research and planning had become a big part of the ritual. It was like a courtship. All the buildup was foreplay. Tonight, though it would all pay off. He felt giddy, almost lightheaded with anticipation.

Carefully he laid out on the dining room table all the items he would need. Rope of course and duct tape. He took a nice chef's knife set out of a shopping bag and laid it on the table. He smiled and hummed a discordant little tune as he organized and packed all the things he might need this evening.

The monster cooked a late lunch of chicken breast cutlet and peas. He showered thoroughly, denying himself his usual bath time self-abuse session. He would save all his seed for her. Thinking about what was to come he had to actively resist the urge. He grabbed his penis roughly and pinched the tip of the head hard and painfully. His erection did ease with some effort. This was the time for calculation and calm. The beast would have his time but not yet.

After showering he changed into the clothes he had laid out on the bed. Khakis and a light blue polo. He sat to put on his black trainers. Simple and comfortable with convenient Velcro straps.

***

The setting sun found him sitting in his parked car several blocks away from the home of his prey. He had made a point to park along the most likely route for her roommates to take when they left for their trip. At 4:15 pm he saw them drive past. To be absolutely sure, the beast waited for another hour before getting out and walking towards the house. He walked at a measured but confident pace. Just another person walking home after work. It was a lively enough neighborhood for a stranger to go unnoticed but not too closely packed for him to have a measure of privacy as he strolled.

It was an older part of town, all hulking Victorian houses with the occasional convenience store or hair salon. Most of the stately old homes had long been converted into multifamily apartments. He wondered what those proper waspy Victorian ghosts thought about the children running down the halls and getting sticky fingers on the wallpaper while unwed mothers chain-smoked and watched trash television in the high-ceilinged parlor. The image of a stuffy old ghost tutting over the threadbare carpets gave him a little chuckle.

There was the occasional manor house that had been left intact. A few had even been painstakingly restored. They were like great polished gems tucked amongst the rust spotted cars, overturned garbage cans and stray cats. It was to one such house that he was heading now.

He casually turned down the narrow alleyway between the buildings that held the garbage cans and entry to the modest yard. A little more than two thirds of the way down the building near the back was a little metal panel. It was around 30 inches wide by 12 inches tall, near to the ground and mostly hidden by a stack of rotting scrap wood. He put on a pair of nitrile gloves and grabbed a longer piece of wood that stuck out of the bottom of the pile and carefully slid the whole pile to one side. The dark cast iron panel was old, and its original ornate filigree was hard to make out. Most people would never notice it or pay it any mind. This forgotten coal shoot was exactly the type of thing that the monster looked for, however. Many older houses had them; —little cast iron doors that led into the basement where deliveries of coal would be deposited directly into the furnace room or coal cellar. In the bygone days of coal burning furnaces these little doors were a great convenience. Most of them now have been bricked over or welded shut. Not this one though. What great luck that it should be overlooked. This was a big one too. Most would have been too small for a man to squeeze through but this one must have also been used to deliver wood or dry goods. Such a jackpot this little door was.

As he wriggled through it and into the dark basement storeroom, he marveled at how the universe seemed to be conspiring to aid in his task.

The monster waked out into the central room of the basement. He had been here before, and it was all quite familiar. He stood in the center of the room among the old paint cans and piles of broken, derelict, antique furniture. Pausing in the dark musty basement he listened—closing his eyes and slowing his breaths, as he opened his ears to the space. A smile unfolded across his lips as he heard the dainty footsteps of his prey. The sound was coming from the front of the house. Pulling up his mental map of the building he guessed that she was walking from the front living room/parlor area. As the footfalls passed overhead and continued to the back corner of the house, he calculated that she was heading into the kitchen.

When she passed over the spot where he stood, a thrill ran through him. There was a shiver of anticipation at her proximity.

The basement filled the entire footprint of the house, and he was able to follow beneath her as she moved through the rooms. The monster listened to his prey making herself dinner. He could hear the clang of pots or pans and the clink of various utensils. He wondered what she was making. It would be her last meal and he hoped it would be a good one.

***

At around 10 pm the distinctive creak of the staircase signaled that his prey was headed upstairs for bed. After waiting an extra bit for her to settle in, he decided it was time.

The monster made his way up the basement stairs that led to a door in a hallway near the kitchen. Stepping lightly on the old wood he made little noise. He took a small knife from his pocket and slid it between the door and jam, lifting the flimsy hook and eye lock and kept the basement door shut. He could have easily just forced the door, but stealth was still important at this stage. He wanted his prey to be completely unaware of his presence until he was looming above her as she lay in bed. The shock and fear were important. She would understand that there was nowhere to run. He wanted to see that realization make her eyes go wide with terror. He wanted to drink in her despair.

When he was just a young monster, he enjoyed a good chase. The prey thought it had a chance. He also got a bit of a thrill from the risk. It was primal and exhilarating. As he got older, he had to leave less to chance. He had learned not to take as many risks. Every hunt taught him something new. That is how he had been able to continue this long. A good monster is a smart monster. Stupid monsters don't last long.

When he entered the hall he took a deep breath, inhaling the scent of the house. It smelled like antique wood lovingly cleaned with orange oil. It smelled like clean linens and home cooked meals. It smelled of tea and herbs and the gentle indistinct perfume that overlays any house occupied by women. Absorbing the olfactory tapestry of the space he detected something else. Something he had not noticed on his previous reconnaissance of the building. It was deep beneath the other smells, and he could not quite identify it. It lurked under the surface and set off a tiny alarm bell in the deepest part of his reptile brain where ancestral memories live. Was it rot? Not exactly. Sharper than that. Mentally he shook himself. Probably just a dead mouse in the wall or a bad pipe or some hidden mold. Who knew in a house this large and old? He needed to stop letting his mind drift. Focus was what was needed.

Tightening the grip on his tool bag he made his way carefully and quietly down the hall and up the stairs, sure to walk near to the wall where floorboards are quieter. Reaching the top of the staircase at the second-floor hall he paused to listen. He could hear the faint electronic buzz and woosh of a white noise machine set to mimic waves crashing on a beach. On a previous visit to the house, he had matched shoes and clothing items in the first room on the right to those he had observed the woman wearing on previous occasions. That door was now open and clearly the source of the recorded ocean sounds. He then reached into his bag to take out the lengths of rope he would soon need.

The monster crept into the room where his prey slept. She lay still with the covers pulled up to her chin and that beautiful hair cascading over the pillow. The beast got close enough to hear her soft exhalation over the soft crashing of waves from the noise machine. So peaceful, so serine. Her skin was so smooth and beautiful. She looked like a sleeping goddess.

She was perfect and now she was his. All the work, all the waiting was about to pay off. This part never got old. He was filled with joy and hunger. His penis began to stiffen. It was time.

He tore the blanket off of her. She had gone to bed in just a t shirt and panties. The beast approved. Her eyes shot open and locked with his. Recognition and terror filled them. She knew immediately what was happening. She took a deep breath and began to open her mouth but before the scream could escape the monster shoved a fistfight of blanket into her face, forcing it into her mouth and preventing her from sounding out an alarm. He roughly turned her body over, forcing her onto her stomach and pressing her face into the pillow. Savagely he punched her twice in the head. Momentarily dazed, her struggles weakened, and he was able to start trying her hands and feet with the rope he had brought. He jumped onto the bed straddling her half naked body. He ran his hand through her hair. Wrapping it around his fist he jerked her head up.

"Are you going to be my good girl?" he asked, breathing heavily into her ear. Her response was a terrified whimper. Savagely he bit into the flesh between her neck and shoulder, sinking his teeth in. He could feel the flesh pop as his teeth met.

She bucked beneath him, and he held her there continuing to press her face into the pillow. The monster kept his teeth firmly clamped on her shoulder. Once the initial convulsive response subsided, he gave a little chew. Again, the prey writhed and squealed.

"Are you going to be my good girl now?" he rasped. He accepted her lack of response.

With one hand still wrapped in her hair he used the other to undo his pants and tear down her underwear.

Usually, he liked to take his time a bit more but this one was different. She awakened in him a hunger that he had not felt in some time. He could not control himself. It was as though he were in a savage trance. This was possibly the best he had ever felt. He lost himself in the violence.

For hours this went on. She stopped putting up any fight. She accepted it. She knew that he owned her now. She gave up and gave herself to him. That proud beautiful queen was his dirty little whore now. A broken doll that he could do whatever he wanted to. Then he noticed that her eyes had gone glassy. He had played too hard with his new toy and broken it. If only he could have restrained himself a bit and made it last. Though the monster preferred to play with living prey, he still knew how to make do with this. Now he owned her entirely. The monster continued on with his depraved acts. Finally exhausted he rolled over to the other side of the bed and lay panting. He pulled the cooling corps into him, spooning it.

* * *

Glancing at the clock on the side table he saw it read 1:59 am. His eyes began to drift shut. Then he felt the body next to him twitch. He heard a gurgling sound coming from its throat. Was she still alive after all? From experience he knew that dead bodies could sometimes spasm, and that gasses trapped in the gut wound could burble up making it sigh.

He rolled the corpse over. She was limp and cold, her dark hair made darker with all the blood. The few bits of skin that were not smeared with blood had gone ashen and dull. He held her head by the jaw and turned it towards him to get a better look. The slack mouth suddenly curled into a smile. Her eyes shot open revealing black orbs that shone with malice. He

31

was frozen with shock. Her mouth opened wide, and she let out a deep hearty chuckle. The mouth that he had left a ruin of broken teeth and gore was now filled with gleaming white fangs like a shark.

With a swift powerful movement, she tore free of her bonds and flipped him over pinning him beneath her. With a hand like an iron clamp around his throat she held him down.

"Are you going to be my good little boy?" she laughed.

What was going on? He fought to understand the situation he now found himself in, struggling under her unyielding grip. How was she this strong? How was she alive? What was she? He glared at her and gritted his teeth, huffing and growling as he tried in vain to wriggle free.

"Oh, my little mouse. How fast your fear turns to anger. You are wasting your energy, but by all means, continue. Your rage will only make you taste better." The creature purred through her mouth of fangs.

Suddenly there were two more figures in the room. A blond girl in her twenties and a redhead with sun kissed freckles—her roommates. Where had they come from? What were they doing here? They too sported black eyes and toothy jackal grins. They took the rest of the rope from his bag and stood him up. One tied his hands behind his back while the other tied a length of rope around his neck like a lead.

That odd smell he had detected earlier was stronger now. He realized it was coming from them. He recognized it. It was the smell of the reptile house at the zoo. It was sweet and sour and spoiled. Like old death and wild beasts.

The woman he had so savagely killed stood before him and stretched her naked, blood-smeared body. It was a deep and luxurious stretch like a cat waking from a particularly good nap. As she did so, bones popped back into place and wounds shrank until they were gone, and her skin was restored.

In his shock, he had stopped struggling. She looked at him with those black orbs and he felt so small. She stood before him and smiled at his emotional shift. The other beasts held him tightly between them. His former prey stepped up to him and without warning sunk her shark teeth into his shoulder. He screamed and slumped but the other two held him up as the creature chewed and slurped at his flesh.

"Don't get greedy sister. He's got to last," one of the other women said. The naked woman released her bite. "Go ahead and take him to the room. I need a shower" she said, wrinkling her nose at bit at the later part.

Gleefully they marched him down to the basement. Their fingers dug into his arms as they jerked him about. How were they so strong? None of this made any sense. He had killed her. How was she back up and moving? What were they?

"We are Lamia," one of the black-eyed women said.

"What?! How did you…" he trailed off in confusion. Had he spoken aloud?

"Shut up you tedious piece of shit," the other creature said peevishly. "We know your mind you mortal twat.".

He was flummoxed. 'Mortal'?. Shock and blood loss from the bite was probably not helping. He tried to kick and struggle but they held him fast.

They pulled and pushed him down into the basement. Sharp stones and grit on the floor dug into his bare feet. They took him to a door at the far end. He had previously taken it to be a storage closet and had not bothered to look inside.

When they opened the door that same stench came rolling out. It was so much more powerful now though. It was the feral stench of a predator's den. Through the door was a small dirt floored room with a wooden chair in the center. The chair was large and sturdy looking and on it sat a pile of rope. Around the chair dozens of candles were lit. The candlelight danced wildly across walls covered in symbols and writing not meant to be seen by human eyes. In the dark corners he could just make out the jagged shapes of bones piled there. Large bones. Human bones.

He knew this was the room in which he would die. He felt his mind collapsing in on itself. His knees went weak at the realization, and he slumped. The Lamia dragged him to the chair.

"Why? Why are you doing this?" He began to sob.

One of the Lamia actually snorted with laughter. "Because you are literally the most disgusting piece of human garbage that we could find," she laughed, as they sat him in the chair and began tying him down with the rope.

Face red with tears and snot beginning to run from his nose he cried out, "Why?"

"Unfortunately for you, but fortunately for your future victims, we need you right now," the light-haired Lamia said.

"There was a time when we could roam the hills feasting on all the succulent little babies. Those were the days," she sighed wistfully.

"Until that stupid covenant we could do whatever we wanted," the redhead continued. They spoke casually as they tied him tightly to the chair.

"Now all the sons and daughters of night have to abide by the rules and mortals are off the menu. Well, sort of anyway. The deal was that we could only act in self-defense. It was so hard at first".

"Then we found out how good a tainted soul could taste," the blonde piped in. "There is a power to it. You feel it when you take a life. That energy gets stored up and fermented in your dark little soul." She patted him on the head.

"The really nasty fucks like you are special. Every vile act you commit makes that concentrated dark energy inside you even more powerful. Your disgusting ass is like a nuclear power plant. That's why we need you in order to call the Master. That is why we brought you here."

"What? You didn't bring me here," he stammered.

"Oh, you think you chose her? You think you have been the one in charge? Look around you darling. She's had you on her hook from day one. We chose you. We have been watching you for a very long time."

He shook his head and tried to blink his confusion away. The Lamia finished with their knots, stepped away and began to disrobe. The redhead looked at her watch.

"It's almost time."

They looked at each other and smiled their shark tooth smiles.

"It's really going to work this time, sister. This one is potent enough," the light-haired Lamia said.

"He better be," the redhead responded with a sigh. "We won't see another alignment for at least a few hundred years."

"It will work sister. Have faith. Everything is in place. We will bring the Master back through and things will go back the way they were."

The third Lamia came through the door. She was still nude though now clean and gleaming with a fierce energy. She lifted her arms high.

"It is time sisters," she proclaimed in a commanding voice.

The three stood around him, opening their toothy jaws wide as they began to make a sound that could have been called song. It was rhythmic and melodic but not in tones that could be produced by human throats. They swayed and undulated around him. The candlelight flickered across their perfect bodies and reflected back at him in their inky black eyes. Their voices rose. They flexed hands that now better resembled claws. The signs and sigils on the walls began to glow with a nauseating green light. They began to slash at him. Twirling around then lashing with a claw to the thigh or a bite to the arm. His screams mingled with the Lamia song until even to him it seemed he was providing the harmonies. The earthen floor before him began to crack. He existed is a world of blood and agony and glowing, screaming sigils. The last thing his conscious mind registered was a massive, clawed hand pushing its way up through the crumbling soil in front of the chair. The Master had come after all.

THE TREE

Jax looked up at the brick front of his new school. It was so big. It was dark and old looking and so unlike the small, neat modern building where his charter school had been back in California. He had no idea what to expect. Sixth grade was scary enough without having also just moved halfway across the country. So far Green Glen West Virginia seemed ok enough.

Their new house was great. It was huge and bright. There were frogs in the pond out back and Biscuits the cat loved chasing grasshoppers in the tall grass. Jax's parents seemed happy too. They seemed more relaxed. The other night he had come downstairs to find both of his moms sitting on the sofa cackling with laughter at some joke they had shared. He couldn't remember the last time he had heard them laugh like that.

The loud ringing of the morning bell shook Jax out of his thoughts. Time to try and find his first class. He gripped his schedule tightly and walked through the heavy antique oak doors of Nathan Bedford Forest Intermediate School.

The day went surprisingly well. He had no idea where anything was, but the staff and kids were really friendly and helpful. His friends back home had warned him about murderous hillbillies and backwoods inbreeds but these people seemed nice. A couple kids did comment on his "Yankee accent" but he didn't think it had been mean spirited. Maybe there was something to this small-town hospitality thing. A couple of the kids had even invited him and his family to church with them. Jax's moms were pretty hard-core atheists with a slight witchy bent so he didn't figure they would go. It was nice to be invited though.

On the bus ride home a pretty girl from his grade sat next to him. It turned out she lived on the same road. She started talking about her church and how great it would be if he would come sometime.

"It's not all stuffy and formal like some places. It's actually fun. We sing and testify and after service we have a cookout and party" she said.

"I don't have like a suit or anything though" Jax said sheepishly.

"Oh, you're silly" she giggled and playfully smacked his arm. "You just come as you are. God only cares about what's inside of you. He won't mind what you're wearing.".

His arm tingled where she had touched him. He would follow this beautiful creature anywhere. He was hypnotized by the way the sunlight through the bus window made her golden hair look as though it were lit from within. As though it was her inner light that was illuminating the world and not the other way around. He almost missed his stop. She touched his arm again to get his attention. Jax was never washing that arm again. He bounced up and started for the front of the bus. He stopped and spun around at the door.

"What's your name? he yelled back at the tiny sun goddess.

"Mary Anne" she called back with a smile like the first day of spring.

"I'm Jax" he said with an awkward wave.

"I know" she answered with a wink.

He jumped down from the bus and quickly walked away so none of the other kids would see his ridiculous grin. He supposed they had all witnessed this awkward exchange leaving the bus and cringed a little.

His big tabby cat Biscuits met him halfway down the drive. The cat walked alongside him meowing loudly about his day, the bell on his little blue-collar jingling as they went. When Jax walked in the house Mom Jenna was standing in the kitchen washing vegetables. Her face lit up when she saw Jax, and she dropped the veggies into the sink and ran over to hug him.

"My precious one! How was your day? Tell me everything! " she beamed.

"It was good actually. I couldn't find any of my classes, but people were super helpful. Do you think I could start going to church? Some of the kids invited me. There's like a special church for kids that's hella cool. Everyone goes and I think I can make friends there" he said.

"Oof kiddo. You know how we feel about church. It's true though that churches are the cultural and community hub in places like this. I guess as long as it's not some crazy snake-handling crap that's going to turn you into a zombie for Jesus." she chuckled the last bit and gave him a hug.

As Jax went up the stairs to his room he realized that he didn't actually know anything about the church. Despite multiple kids telling him about the church's youth services, none of them had given any actual description of the service or their specific beliefs. He REALLY hoped that it wasn't anything crazy. He realized though that if Marry Anne was there, he would happily gabber away in tongues and pet any snake she wanted. If it was too nuts, then he just wouldn't go back. He opened his backpack and settled in on his bed with Biscuits to get some homework done.

***

The next couple of days went on about the same. Jax knew where his classes were now though. He was definitely making friends. When he said he was planning to attend church that Sunday it seemed like every kid in the school was suddenly his buddy. Like he had performed the secret handshake and was now part of the community. When he told Mary Anne on the way home that he got the ok to go to church with her, she took his hand in both of hers and squeezed it. All the light and warmth in the world was contained in her smile. He would do anything to see that smile. Jax may have only had a twelve-year old's understanding of love and romance, but he understood that this was how it starts. There was a tiny logical part of his mind that understood that the power she now had over him could be a very dangerous thing. That little voice however was entirely drowned out by the angel trumpets that he heard every time he looked at her.

Sunday couldn't come fast enough. Jax walked to Mary Anne's to ride with her and her family to church. He had decided to wear his nicest casual clothes. He had spent the night and half the morning agonizing over the perfect balance of stylish and effortless. He had to look his best but without seeming to have tried too hard. In the end he went with a newer pair of black jeans and a short-sleeve button up that his moms said made him look handsome. Then to tie it all together he wore his brand-new suede skate shoes. By the time Jax reached the end of his own driveway, he realized his mistake. His shoes and pants were covered in road dust. This was just perfect. She was going to think he was an idiot. That didn't stop him though. He wouldn't miss this opportunity.

It wasn't long before he reached the mailbox shaped like a billy goat that Mary Anne had told him marked her driveway. Her house was set far back from the road like many of the properties in the area. As he walked, he noticed her family's herd of goats chomping away at the undergrowth on either side of the driveway. Maybe after church he could come back and pet them. Could you pet a farm goat? Were farm animals nice? He remembered the petting zoos his moms would take him to when he was little. These goats were definitely not the same as the cute little hand raised ones at the petting zoo. They were big and rangy. They stared at him with large alien eyes that managed somehow to seem both blank and judgmental. He saw a dark flash between the trees. What was that? It was kind of dark in the trees here. The forest was thick and dense. He suddenly felt a chill and wasn't sure if it was a breeze or something from within. He shook off the feeling and continued.

After a couple more minutes the trees opened up to reveal a small barnyard and white farmhouse that looked like something from a painting. Of course she lived in a perfect house. A big shaggy black dog got up from the porch and padded up to him. It didn't bark or growl. It walked up, sniffed him, gave his hand a little lick then seemed to escort him to the door. As he stepped up onto the tidy porch, he noticed an ornate folk-art wreath on the door. September seemed a bit early for wreaths. There was a pattern of sticks running through the center. They formed something like a star but not a star. He had never seen anything quite like it. Before he could give it any more thought, the door swung open.

Mary Anne was standing there in a pale floral sundress and white cardigan. Every thought left his head. She was so stunning. She smiled at him and he wasn't sure if he could make his legs work. He stammered something like "Hello". " as he took it all in. Then a tall handsome man in khakis and a button up shirt walked up behind her.

"Hey there big chief. I'm Mary Anne's father Paul. But you can call me Mr. Simon," he said, extending a big, calloused hand out for a shake.

Wanting to make a good impression he found his voice and said, "Nice to meet you, Sir. My name is Jax," taking Mr. Simon's hand and giving it the best shake he could muster.

"Joanne! The boy is here. Are you ready?" Mr. Simon turned and bellowed into the house.

"Yes, darl'n I'm coming. Hold your horses."

Mrs. Simon stepped up behind Mr. Simon holding a covered casserole dish that smelled amazing. She was a beautiful woman. An older version of Mary Anne. The matching outfit probably helped but the hair and facial features were nearly identical. While Mary Anne's chest had yet to develop, he could not help but wonder if she would inherit her mother's more than ample bosom the way she had her fine golden hair and button nose. He forced himself to look Mrs. Simon in the face and resist the draw of her breasts barely contained under the thin sundress.

"Nice to meet you, Mrs. Simon" he said.

"Oh gosh honey, call me Joanne. Now let's git off this porch and in the car before we get ourselves late to church" she said with a laugh and smile.

They all walked down the porch and to the SUV parked out front. As they got in and got buckled up Joanne asked, "Where are your mother and father sweetie? Where they busy today?"

"Oh, my moms aren't religious" replied Jax.

"Moms? Pleural?" Joanne asked, a little strain creeping into her voice. "Oh, I see" she said. "Well god loves all his children. Even the wayward ones."

A smile returned to her face though this time it looked more brittle and less welcoming.

The awkward silence was soon broken with small talk about the weather and questions about how Jax was settling in. The church wasn't in town. Rather it was down a series of dirt roads taking them further and further into the middle of nowhere. The last road made him thankful that they were in a SUV. Jax wasn't sure a standard sedan would have been able to navigate the ruts and bumps. Seemed kind of weird to have a church this far out. Just then, a man with a long beard stepped out of the trees and onto the road ahead of them and began walking down the dirt track. No one reacted. As they went on more and more people began walking out of the woods and onto the road. Men and women. Single people, couples, and families. Jax noticed that some were a bit disheveled looking and had old fashioned clothes. Some were even going barefoot. He chalked it up to rural culture. This was West Virginia after all. This was a world that he didn't know about and he had always been taught to be respectful of other people's cultures and lifestyles. It still kind of creeped him out though. Where were they coming from? How far had they walked? Man, Christians are fucking weird.

When they finally got to the church Jax did not feel particularly reassured. The building was like something out of one of his apocalyptic video games. It was a small one room country style church with a tall steeple that listed to one side. What paint hadn't flaked off the ancient wood siding was an off-white faded grey. Instead of a cross, another wreath with that odd configuration of sticks hung on the door.

Mary Anne must have sensed his apprehension because she then put a hand on his arm and beaming at him said "I'm so glad you decided to come. It means a lot to me".

They parked alongside several other vehicles in a dirt parking lot to the side of the building. When Jax got out he noticed that behind the church, just past the tree line there were more buildings and some standing stones, drenched in shadow and leaning drunkenly. Was it an old graveyard?

"You coming?" Mary Anne called after him.

He tore his eyes away from the dark trees and ran to join Mary Anne and the crowd shuffling into the church. He recognized quite a few of his classmates in the crowd. They smiled and waved at him, and he returned the gesture.

It was much larger inside than he expected. Joanne set her casserole next to dozens of other dishes and baskets of food on a table by the door. They followed Mr. Simon to the second pew on the left and filed in to sit. For the most part the inside looked how you would imagine a small country church to look. There were rows of wooden pews facing a small central platform and podium. There was a piano to the side where a sweet looking old woman sat sorting through sheet music. It lacked the traditional cross at the front but instead there was a giant painting of a tree whose twisting branches reached onto the ceiling. Maybe this particular brand of Christianity had a surprisingly new age bent?

Everyone looked so excited. It was a joyful atmosphere. Once they were all seated the woman at the piano began to play and the room quieted down. Then the tallest, thinnest man Jax had ever seen entered the front of the church from some previously unseen door. He stepped up to the podium with his arms raised and a grin that stretched painfully across his too thin face.

"Welcome brothers and sisters!" he bellowed.

"Blessed is the blood within!" the congregation all responded in unison.

"Hail and praise him" the preacher said back.

"Praise be the branches that reach and the roots that bind," everyone chanted back.

"I see we have some new blood with us today," the preacher said, turning wild piercing eyes at Jax. "Welcome young Jax. We are excited to have you here.".

The attention made Jax uncomfortable. He didn't like being singled out, but he decided to be a good sport —nodding his head as he smiled sheepishly.

"As you all know, with the harvest festival coming soon it is important to spread the good word and to collect and deliver your tithings to the Lord. If you have not yet secured your tithing, then I encourage you to do so this week.".

He pointed a too long gnarled finger towards Paul and Joanne.

"Our beloved kin the Simons have done well spreading the word and have promised to bring two goats in for the festival. It is through this kind of generosity that we nourish our community," the preacher went on.

He continued to speak of sacred blood and the love of god and sacrifices. Jax definitely thought it was weird and at some points a little disturbing. Having no real context though, he didn't dwell on the words too much. He kind of zoned out, staring past the preacher to the tree painted behind him. He let his eyes unfocus a bit. Could he see tiny faces hidden in the painted texture of the bark? It was so detailed that he could easily imagine the branches swaying slightly in the breeze. Wait… did he just see them actually move some? No. He was just starting to daydream. Must have been.

Jax could tell by the rhythm of the preacher's speech that he was wrapping up.

"Remember to have all your tithes in by the new moon next week. Praise and hail him brothers and sisters. "

And the congregation once more responded, "Praise the branches that reach and the roots that bind.".

The priest reached his impossibly long thin arms out to either side. "Let us go to feast and fellowship. "

At that, everyone stood up and began to shuffle towards the back where the tables of food sat. There were already a couple ladies over there ready to hand out plates and dole out mounds of potato salad.

The food was amazing. He had never had anything so delicious. Something told him that words like low-fat, vegan, or gluten-free might as well have been a foreign language here. Standing in the church yard eating this bounty and chatting up Mary Anne and the other children, he decided that he didn't care how weird and creepy the preacher and his sermon were. He would absolutely do this every week. He felt really comfortable and accepted. He had never had an easy time making friends and hadn't really had any close ones at his old school. He could definitely understand the draw that church had.

They were there into the afternoon. The little children running around while the adults caught up on gossip and news of the day. Jax and his classmates were walking around the edge of the woods talking about classes and teachers and what television shows they had been watching. As they passed near the buildings and stones in the woods that Jax had seen earlier he asked the other kids about them.

"That's where we have youth group. You can come next week if you want" a dark-haired boy who Jax thought was maybe named Hunter said.

"What do you do there?" asked Jax.

"Mostly we talk and share and plan tithing and events," said a tall girl, whose name he didn't know.

Joanne came and found them soon after and ushered them off to the SUV. Jax and Mary Anne chatted and giggled the whole way home. Before he knew it, they were pulling up at his house. His mothers came outside to say hello when the Simons pulled up. Instead of chatting however Joanne gave a wave like flick of her hand and offered that brittle smile and nothing else. They drove back down the driveway and away without saying hello.

"Well, that was fucking rude," Mom Maxine grumbled under her breath.

"Mom stop. They're nice," Jax said defensively. His moms exchanged a look and they all walked inside.

Jax flopped down on his bed and took a short nap. When they woke him for dinner, he was surprised not to see Biscuits laying with him. His cat always turned up for a nap.

"Have you guys seen Biscuits?" he asked when got downstairs.

Mom Jenna handed him a stack of plates and silverware to set out in the table and answered, "Not since this morning. He wasn't upstairs with you? Probably out chasing mice or something."

When he hadn't turned up by 9 pm Jax went outside with the container of cat treats and shook them. Biscuits knew this sound well and it never failed to bring that big tabby running and mewing to be fed. He wanted so badly to hear his little bell jingle and see him running up. He had heard there were coyotes out here, but Jax didn't want to think about that. After several minutes of shaking the treats with no results, he decided to call in a night and shuffled dejectedly to bed.

In the morning he set out a can of his cat's favorite wet food and made his mothers promise to keep an eye out.

"Maybe he just found a girlfriend, " Mamma Maxine tried to joke.

It fell flat when she saw Jax's face. She pulled him in for a hug.

"We'll find him sweetheart. Don't worry."

He slogged his way to the end of the driveway and waited for the bus.

When he got on and sat down next to Mary Anne, she noticed his mood and asked, "What's the matter?"

"I can't find my cat. He didn't come in last night and I'm really worried about him," he replied.

"What does he look like?" she asked. "I'll keep an eye out and let the other neighbors know. He's probably just exploring."

"He's a big male grey tabby," Jax said. "He has a blue collar with a bell on it. He's super friendly and his name is Biscuits. I've had him since I was little. He's kind of my best friend."

Mary Anne took his hand and held it. Her face was the very picture of care and sympathy.

"We'll get you and your cat back together. I promise "she said earnestly.

***

That week was so hard for Jax. All he could think about was his cat. Biscuits was his first and only pet. He had never dealt with death or loss like this. He kept telling himself that his cat was probably sitting on a pillow and drinking cream at some old lady's house like a jerk. In his heart of hearts, he knew better though. He pushed the darker thoughts as deep down as he could. Hopefully youth group at the church would take his mind off of it.

Sunday morning finally came again and Jax was sitting in the kitchen having breakfast with his moms. Momma Maxine put her fork down and looked at Jax very seriously.

"Are you sure you want to keep going to that church? They don't seem very inclusive and what you told me about the sermon sounds like some crazy fire and brimstone stuff. I'm worried about it," she said.

"If you guys came to the church you would see it's not bad and they could get to know you too. Plus, I get to be with Mary Anne. Her family is great too," Jax replied defensively.

"Honey, are you sure they aren't just trying to convert you? Cults and religious groups are always trying to get recruits. They get cute girls to flirt with boys and get them to join thinking it's a way to get in good with the girl. It's all mind control. We are really worried that might be happening," Mom Jenna said as she started to reach across the table to take Jax's hand.

He yanked his hand away from her and looked at her with shocked anger.

"You have no idea what you're talking about! I can't believe you don't think a girl would like me. They don't have any kind of agendas, they're just nice. Mary Anne really likes me, and you just can't stand that I'm hanging out with anyone but you! You think you're so open minded, but you think they are in a cult just because they don't have the same beliefs as you!"

Jax was starting to yell.

Mamma Maxine stood up.

"Don't you take that tone with us! We are trying to protect you!" she yelled back.

"Well you can stop! I'm a Christian now and I love Mary Anne! You can't control what I believe in!" he shot back, then got up from the table and stormed out the front door.

Mom Jenna started to cry so Maxine put an arm around her shoulder.

"We knew puberty would come sooner or later and the asshole phase would start. Just never figured backwoods Christianity would be how he rebelled."

They both had to laugh a little at that. Maxine kissed the top of Jenna's head and said "He's going to stomp off to Mary Anne's house and do his youth group thing and calm down. He's a smart kid. He's learning a new thing and that's ok. Once the newness wears off, he will drop it like he did with his fedora stage last year."

"I just hope he doesn't get his heart broken too bad, " Jenna replied.

"He will. And we will be here to hold him when he does," Maxine said back. They stayed there in the kitchen embracing.

***

Jax stomped down the driveway towards Mary Anne's house. He was so angry. He wanted to punch a tree or something. His parents were so stupid. Who did they think they were?! Had he really said that he loved Mary Anne? Maybe she did too. He was pretty sure that he loved her. Would it be too soon to say it? Was she his girlfriend? They hadn't talked about it but it kind of seemed that way. Maybe after youth group he would ask her officially to be his girlfriend? His anger was replaced by excitement and nervousness. Thinking of her always made him feel better. Once he calmed down a bit, he started to feel bad about what he had said to his moms. They just didn't understand though. If they would only come to church and get to know everyone it would be fine.

Before he knew it, he was knocking on the door of the cute little farmhouse. Once again, the big black dog had escorted him to the porch. He had learned the other day that his name was Bear. He gave Bear a pat on the head and Mary Anne opened the door. Her face lit up when she saw him. The rest of the world melted away and all that existed was her light.

"You're early! Did you have breakfast yet? Come in. Come in," she said in a rush.

"Yeah. I got into a big fight with my parents this morning and didn't get to actually eat anything," he said a sulkily.

"Oh no! That's terrible. You come in and eat with us.".

She put a hand on his arm and led him into a bright clean kitchen with red gingham curtains. Her parents were seated at little oak table eating pancakes and sipping orange juice. There was a woman there too. Well, a girl maybe. She was older than him and Mary Anne but much younger than her parents. She had dreadlocks and wore heavy braided hemp jewelry. Did Mary Anne have an older teenage sister he didn't know about?

"Well look who's early, "Mary Anne's mother said with a smile.

She stood up, fetched a plate and silverware, and made another place at the table for Jax. She piled his plate high with pancakes and bacon and eggs. These people definitely knew how to do breakfast right.

"I'm glad you could join us, Jax," Mr. Simon said. "We have another guest as well. Meet Starla. We saw her out hitch hiking yesterday and invited her to come have a hot meal and a soft bed. She's joining us for services today as well," he continued.

For her part Starla smiled around a mouthful of pancakes and waved at Jax. He was amazed that these people would take in a stranger like that. They really were the nicest people ever. Jax felt a little flash of anger at how his mothers had talked about them.

"What were you fighting with your parents about?" Mary Anne asked Jax.

"They don't want me going to church with you guys. They don't understand" Jax said churlishly.

"The good book does say to honor your mother and father but I'm not sure about mother and MOTHER, "Joanne said with a laugh. The Simons all laughed. Jax joined in despite himself. Starla looked a bit uncomfortable and just focused on her plate.

"We are family in the Lord now sweetie. Don't you worry about a thing." Joanne leaned forward to take Jax's hand as she spoke. Once again, he had to make a very conscious effort to look her in the face and not down at the cleavage that was now visible through the neckline of her dress.

***

They finished breakfast and headed to church. On the long ride there, Starla regaled everyone with stories of her life and the road. She had been in Colorado working at a pot farm. Her boyfriend had kicked her out and she decided to hitch hike to Maine to live on some nudist colony and grow magic mushrooms.

"Isn't it super cold in Maine? Can you be a nudist in the snow?" Jax asked.

Before Starla could answer, Joanne said a little shrilly, "Well maybe we can help you find a different path."

With every word of Starla's story Joanne's face had become more and more pinched. At one point Jax wondered if it would simply collapse in on its self in consternation. Mr. Simon had been silent, but his brow was heavily furrowed.

They pulled up to the church and both adults whole demeanor changed. Their faces relaxed into smiles and their eyes went bright. The speed of the switch disturbed Jax a little. As before, Mrs. Simon deposited her casserole dish with the others and they filed into the same pew. There were more people here this time though. A lot of unfamiliar faces. Almost like all of the families had brought a guest.

The preacher came out and the congregation went through the same call and response as before. He talked about the special new moon service and thanked everyone for bringing a guest. Mr. Simon had acted like it had been a coincidence that he had picked up Starla but the way the preacher was talking made Jax wonder if that was true. She looked uncomfortable. Jax thought she might be coming to the same conclusion.

The sermon was soon over and it was time for food. Apparently Starla was a vegetarian and she was having a hard time finding food that didn't have meat in it. She ended up just eating pie and Jello. Some older girls were talking to her. It seemed like she found some friends. Everyone was having a good time. The adults and older children played cornhole and horseshoes while the little children played tag and hunted for caterpillars.

After a while Jax went for a walk with Mary Anne and the others from their grade. He had to find a way to get her alone so he could ask her to be his girlfriend officially. There were a couple new children with them. They were "guests" like Starla. One was a boy's cousin from Missouri and the other was a kind of surly foster child.

The sun was getting low in the sky and Jax knew he needed to make his move soon or he would lose his nerve.

"Hey Mary Anne? Can we go for a walk together? Just us? I want to talk to you," he asked. The other children giggled and exchanged knowing looks.

"Of course we can" she replied taking his hand and pointing her nose in the air in response to the others' laughter.

She led him towards the woods as he babbled on about her beauty and his feelings. He vaguely registered that they were walking towards the creepy looking buildings and stone markers. As they approached, he noticed that the stones were actually a ring around the buildings. They weren't gravestones either. They were rough, irregularly cut, and had symbols carved into them. He needed to stay focused though. He kept gushing on about how he had never felt this way and that he could get her a promise ring if she wanted. He said he would do anything.

He was so focused on getting his feelings out that it wasn't until she stopped walking that he realized she hadn't yet made any response. He hadn't really noticed where they were either. And what was that smell? Was there a dead deer out here somewhere? They were standing in a ring of buildings within the ring of stones. In the center was a giant tree. He couldn't tell what kind. It was huge and twisting. She turned towards him and took both his hands in hers. It was then that he saw the source of the smell. How had he missed it? Had he really been that deeply under her spell? He thought about what his mothers had said. He loved them so much. As he looked at the tree and all the corpses of animals and humans hanging from the branches and piled at its base, he knew that he would never see his parents again. He saw Starla crumpled among the roots with her throat slit. He saw a small ruined bloody shape that had been cruelly nailed in place about halfway up the trunk of the tree. Tears started streaming down his face when he recognized the blue collar and bell still attached to its neck.

"I love you too Jax" Mary Anne said still holding both his hands. "But I can't be your girlfriend. You belong to the Lord and he is very hungry."

HOUSE OF THE WOLF

I open my mouth wide and scream

I scream until my throat tears open.

I scream until the little beast comes

She has teeth that gnash and a face that snarls

She screams for me

She continues the howl long after I lose my voice

They cower before her sound

They run from her teeth that bite

They did not know she lived there

I am the tiny breath that contains eons

I am the house of all things

I try my best not to collapse under my own weight

<u>CULLING SEASON</u>

Chapter 1

Yagga's feet were killing her. Trudging through the thick scrubland had proved to be even more work than she had anticipated. She knew she had seen a bush of Feversbaine near here before, she just couldn't remember exactly where. They had walked half a day to get here and now the sun was getting low. Her thick, mammoth-hide sandals were scant protection against the sharp stones here in the valley, and the old woman's bones ached from exertion. Yagga muttered to herself and spat in frustration. She needed to calm down and focus or she would never find that stupid bush.

"Is this it Mamma Yagga?" Flira called from a few yards away. The young girl held up a small branch for Yagga to see. She squinted her aged eyes to study the plant in the girl's hand.

"No, my dear, but you're not far off. The one we need has darker berries and the leaves have streaks of red through them.".

Yagga turned her face to the sky and took a deep calming breath.

"Please Ysmiir help me see" she whispered in prayer to the Goddess of healing plants.

Just then a little bird flitted into view. It was a Blue Piper, the bird most used by Ysmiir for omens and messages. The little bird flapped and circled over Yagga, seeming to make sure that it had been seen and recognized. She watched it fly off to the south several yards and then it was out of sight.

"Follow me girl. I think we have it" Yagga called out to Flira as she trundled in the direction that the bird had flown.

They crested a small rise and there it was. The little bird was perched neatly on the top of a giant bush of Feversbaine. The late afternoon sun reflected on the bird's feathers making it look like a shining blue gem come to life. It gazed steadily at the women with bright, intelligent eyes and gave a happy chirp before flying off. A wide smile filled Yagga's face bringing out every line and crease that her advanced age and wisdom had earned her. She muttered the customary thanks to Ysmiir and touched the pouch around her neck that contained sacred herbs and a tiny carved idol of her patron Goddess. Flira stood with her eyes and mouth wide.

"Did…did that bird just show you the bush? Was that Ysmiir? Is that really Feversbaine?" she prattled on in shock.

"Yes, child yes" Yagga said, still smiling widely. "I asked and she helped. She doesn't always act so directly but this is important."

Flira had been her apprentice for only a few seasons and this was her fist true sight of a God or Goddess at work. One day she would be granted the gift of Speech but that was some time away now.

"Hurry now girl. Let's gather all we can carry" Yagga commanded, snapping the girl out of her awe.

They both produced short, curved knives from their belts and began filling their rough woven sacks with the precious plant.

"Get leaves and berries girl. Line the bottom with the leaves and put the berries in the middle of the sack to protect them. Can't afford for them to get damaged before we can get back."

They helped each other secure the bundles to their backs with strips of rawhide then headed back up toward their village in the hills. Under normal circumstances Yagga would have opted to camp for the night, taking time to rest while her apprentice tended the fire and made supper for them. This though, was an urgent errand.

***

These precious leaves and berries would mean the difference between life and death for Arma's two little boys. They were only a season away from their first naming day and still fragile little creatures. Time was a luxury they could not risk wasting if the babes were to have any chance at survival. Yagga had already tried the normal remedies, but nothing could get their fever to subside. It had started just like the normal autumn chills that came every year, with a little snuffle, a low fever, and the general crankiness of a sick child. She had her herb stores stocked and ready for the yearly sicknesses that come with the change in the weather. After administering her usual remedies, however, nothing had improved. In fact, it had gotten worse. Their tiny bodies convulsed with violent coughing that rattled deep and wet within their chest. The fever rose in them until touching them was like laying a bare hand on a cooking stone. While Yagga knew that it was no strange thing for the very young or the very old to succumb to illness, she felt in her belly that this was something else. Even the Feversbaine that she had in her stores did nothing. It was old and had likely lost some of its potency, however. It should have done SOMETHING though, she thought. Yagga decided that first thing in the morning she and her apprentice would head out to gather some of the plant. Feversbaine when fresh was an incredibly powerful medicine.

The next morning as she was preparing to leave for her herb gathering expedition, Yagga heard that same deep wet cough coming from Tresnal's hut. She marched right over and threw back his door flap. Tresnal was lying down, wrapped in furs while his wife held a drinking gourd to his lips. Yagga could see that his lips were flecked with bloody spittle. They both looked up at Yagga with pleading eyes.

"How long has he been ill? Why did you not fetch me before it got so bad?!" Yagga barked at the other woman.

"He is only just now so poorly, Mother Yagga. He had a sore head and some tiredness last evening then he woke up early with this terrible cough. What is it Mother? Can you help him?"

The old medicine woman did her best to keep her composure. How could it have advanced so quickly?

"Keep giving him water and don't let him out of his furs. I will come back with strong medicine for him" she told the distraught woman curtly, then left the hut to find her apprentice.

She frantically searched her mental repository for some clue about what this illness could be. It was obvious that it was spreading. Yagga knew how fast these types of sicknesses could leap from hut to hut. She needed to get ahead of it. She needed strong medicine, and she needed it fast.

***

By the time elder and apprentice got back to their village, the waxing moon was high in the sky and Yagga was leaning heavily on Flira's arm. The village was quiet save for coughing coming from the huts and the occasional muffled sound of weeping. There was a palpable air of sorrow on the wind.

They went straight to work in Yagga's hut, mashing berries into paste and brewing tea with the leaves of the lifesaving plant. The two visited each home administering the medicine that they had worked all day to procure. First, they went to Arma's home to see that her baby boys got the first dose. The children were so weak at this point that they were beyond even crying and just lay panting with glassy eyes. Their smooth chestnut skin had gone grey and dull. Yagga blessed the boys in the name of Ysmiir and asked the Goddess' protection for them. They gave the medicine to every member of the village, sick or not. Though as they went to each door, the two women found that just in the day that had passed, there were more sick people than healthy ones.

When the task was done, they returned to Yagga's hut to pray. She called on Cartomi and Mayanni, the great mother and father, to watch over her people. She prayed to the warrior god Tegomny to slay the evil that had befallen them. She prayed and sang the songs of Calling all through the night. Flira fetched water for Yagga and brewed a special tea so that the old woman could keep her energy up.

When the sun began to peak out from the horizon, both women were swaying with exhaustion. As the rays of light began to filter through the little window above Yagga's alter, it was suddenly blotted out. There was a giant bird sitting on the ledge. It had black feathers that shone like obsidian and eyes that glowed like smoldering coals. Flira cried out in terror at the sight. The bird cocked its head at her quizzically and made a tutting noise. Yagga narrowed her eyes at the creature and spat at the ground.

"Get out of here you old thief" Yagga said with a shewing motion. "I gave them the medicine and Ysmiir blessed it so you may leave now."

The great bird made the tutting noise again but now at Yagga. "I steal nothing child. No need for insults just because you are unhappy at my arriving" the bird spoke in a tone that made Flira think of dark, warm water.

While Yagga seemed annoyed or even angry, Flira was transfixed. She was terrified but fascinated. She had heard that medicine women spoke directly to the Gods but had not thought it would be so literal and direct. For Flira this was an earth-moving moment but Yagga was acting simply as though an unpleasant neighbor had come calling. What is this creature? Flira thought to herself. Then the bird turned its fiery gaze and looked directly at Flira.

"I am Bockdi, child. I am the one that helps the dead to cross the River" he said in his dark silky voice.

"He is a thief! He takes our people away into the Night Lands" Yagga spat.

"Don't be churlish daughter, " he said calmly. "It is simply the way things are. Just as the grass comes and goes in its season, so it is for you and your people. I am merely here to assist those who need help crossing the River."

Yagga scoffed loudly and hurried out of the hut.

"We shall see!" she shouted back as she marched towards Arma's hut to see to the sick young boys. "Fetch the water gourds Flira and be quick" she barked.

Flira turned her head in response to Yagga's shouted orders and when she turned back the great bird was gone. She did as she was told, and she went with Yagga to tend the sick.

***

When they arrived at Arma's home, it was silent. It appeared that Arma was sleeping soundly in her furs with the two babes nestled close. A moment's inspection however revealed the tragic truth. All three were ashen grey and completely still. Yagga stood in a moment of reverence for the dead and allowed herself the indulgence of a single tear before hurrying out the entrance flap to see to the rest of her charges. It was soon clear that the Feversbaine had done no good. The women worked endlessly tending to the sick and comforting the grieving.

The next several days were a blur of death and despair. The sounds of hacking coughs and weeping became as ubiquitous as cricket and bird song. Nothing Yagga did seemed to help. Those that were still well enough to be up and about spent what energy they had digging shallow graves for the mounting dead. Yagga kept praying. They all did. One of the men sacrificed a great Aurochs in hopes that the gods would spare his wife. No aid was given. The gods were conspicuously silent. Even old Bockdi did not show his beak again.

***

Yagga asked herself, *How could their Gods have abandoned them?* They had been a devout people. They had always praised the Gods and made the appropriate offerings. Yagga could always depend on them for good council in times of need. But now there was not so much as a subtle sign. It made Yagga furious. Her people were falling like leaves from the trees and there was nothing she could do. She had tended to four generations of her people. She delivered them as babies and held their hand when Bockdi came for them. She had set the bones of the men when a mammoth hunt went badly. She gave them comfort and council and interceded with the Gods on their behalf. Now she could only watch as they coughed their insides out and fever boiled them alive. She'd had enough.

She sat by the big fire circle in the center of the village nursing a gourd of warm tea, and she began to weep. It started slow and quiet but soon built to a torrent. She found herself on her knees before the flames of the central fire, sobbing and screaming. Yagga wailed her sorrows into the night. She pulled her hair and tore at her own face. Clearly mad with grief for her people. No one would approach her and the few souls who still breathed offered her no comfort. She exhausted what energy she had and collapsed into the dirt. The old woman had not slept in days and drifted swiftly into a deep slumber.

* * *

In her sleep, Yagga knew no rest, however. She found herself walking a mossy path through a shimmering wood. The stench of sickness and death that had filled the waking world was replaced by a soft breeze filled with the scent of flowers and growing things. She walked to a clearing where two figures, a man and a woman, lounged on a bed of flowers. Beautiful birds of all colors flitted about them and filled the air with music. The man had a thick black beard and wore a crown of Thornvine. The woman had dark, wavy hair long enough to cover her body like a cloak and resting atop her head was a crown of white snow flowers. Yagga knew without being told that she was in the presence of Cartomi and Mayanni, the mother and father of all. She fell to her knees and bowed her head in reverence.

"No child. Rise and sit with us" a voice like a cool breeze said into her ear.

She looked up to see the two smiling and gesturing for her to come and sit with them. She did as she was asked. Despite her advanced years, Yagga felt like a little child sitting with them. While their size did not seem unusual when Yagga had been some ways away, now that she was before them, she could see that they were at least three times larger than her and her people.

"I have been praying Mother and Father. I have been calling for you" she began to cry.

"Do not cry so child. It will all be as it should, "said Mayanni and she stroked Yagga's cheek with her large but graceful hand.

"So, you will save them?" Yagga choked out, her eyes looking hopeful through the tears.

"No child. All things have their season and their purpose. Sometimes a tragedy must come to make way for a future good. It is the way of things," said Cartomi in a calm fatherly tone.

"What good could the death of my people possibly do?!" Yagga nearly screamed.

Were the Gods just going to abandon them?! Or worse yet…had the Gods orchestrated this on purpose? Rage filled her.

"This is the way of things. A leaf falling sets off a chain of events that ensures that next year's hunt goes well. You and your village are but one tree in a great forest. Take joy in coming home to us. It is not a punishment," Mayanni said calmly.

"Do not speak to me like a child! I am a woman grown old enough to know how precious life is. I may not have long left before I cross the River but I will not allow my people to do so before it is their time. We have loved and worshiped you and you care not if we live or die. What parent would willfully kill their own children? 'Mother and father' indeed. You are not who I thought you were, "Yagga sneered. "I seek your counsel no more.".

Yagga woke with a start to see Flira kneeling beside her shaking her awake. Yagga sat bolt upright. "They have abandoned us. They did this to us on purpose. That is why our prayers go unanswered, "Yagga began to sob again.

"Is there nowhere else to turn? Is there no one else to ask?" Flira pleaded.

Suddenly Yagga stopped crying. Her mouth was set with determination and her eyes took on a far way look. She turned to stare into the darkness beyond the village.

Without taking her eyes away from the shadows she asked, "Have they buried Hesna's little daughter yet?"

"No Mother Yagga, I don't think so. Why?".

"Now is not the time to question me. Fetch the babe and bring it to my hut," Yagga said flatly then got up and started walking towards her home.

It was not long before Flira walked into the hut carrying the deceased infant wrapped in a hide.

"I told her I was taking her baby to bury it for her," Flira said in a faraway voice.

"Set it here," Yagga said, gesturing to her altar. It had been cleared of all but a knife carved of black stone with a bone handle. A knife the Flira had never seen in all her years apprenticing under the old woman. "Tonight, we call on the Others," Yagga said as she opened the wrapping, revealing the form of the little girl's corpse. She had been a full turn of seasons past her naming day and had begun to speak some words. Now she was dead and cold; forever silenced. The moonlight shone through the small window making the dead girl's already grey skin look even paler.

"You can't. You said we can never…" Flira started.

"We have no choice, "Yagga cut her off. She spoke with a mixture of shame and determination.

She took the knife in her hand and held it up high. Yagga spoke the words of Calling. Flira watched the moonlight dance on the black blade and thought she could see shapes moving within the carved stone. Then she realized that Yagga was no longer speaking in a language that she understood. It sounded guttural and harsh. This was not a ritual that Flira had been taught. She wanted to run. This was wrong. Despite her fear, she was unable to move. The old woman continued muttering in that strange tongue as her gnarled hands set to work with the blade. She pressed it to the soft flesh of the child's corpse. She carved a symbol like a star, but not. It hurt Flira's eyes to look at it too long. The dead flesh began to bleed. That shouldn't be possible, thought Flira. The dead don't bleed. Yagga's mumbling grew louder, more vehement. She spat the words. She growled and screeched them. Black blood began to pour fourth from the symbol carved on the infant's chest. Again, Yagga took the black blade in hand. She used it to cut a piece of flesh from the tiny corpse's thigh. In abject horror, Flira watched as Yagga placed the strip of flesh in her mouth and began to chew it. She closed her eyes as she chewed. She swallowed.

The world went black. The moon no longer shone. The reflected light of the village fire was snuffed out. It was silent too. No crickets or breeze. It was as though someone had put a sack over her head. Suddenly two points of light appeared. Green glowing orbs like two great fireflies. They blinked. Flira did not even realize she was screaming until Yagga grabbed her arm roughly and yelled for her to be silent.

"What do you need of me?" whispered a voice in the darkness. The words were stilted like the creature was not used to the act of speech.

"The Gods have sent sickness to my people. They ignore my pleas and refuse to give aid. They no longer love us," Yagga said with a quavering voice.

"You know there is a price for my help," the voice behind the glowing eyes spoke.

"Any price is better than this. I would give anything to save my people from this horrible death," pleaded Yagga.

"And you speak for your people?" asked the Other.

"Yes. They are mine to care for and I speak on their behalf with the Gods," said Yagga, her back straightening a bit.

"Very well. From this moment your people will not be touched by death. Your lost babes will be restored to you. Your people will carry on across the land and spread far and wide and never know the sleep of death," hissed the voice. The glowing eyes blinked out, and light and sound rushed back into the hut like a strong wind.

The women were both dazed by the experience and could only look at each other. When the noises outside coalesced, they could make out the sound of raised voices coming from the village around them. They both started for the entrance flap, but stopped dead when they heard a gurgling choking sound coming from behind them on the altar. The previously lifeless body of the toddler was writhing and gasping for breath. Yagga dashed to the little pale creature and scooped her up in her arms.

"She is back! The Others kept their promise, and we are saved!" Yagga spoke through tears of joy.

She cradled the little girl to her chest. The child struggled and flailed in Yagga's arms. She lifted her tiny head to look up at Yagga. It was then that Flira realized that the child had not been gasping for breath. It was gnashing its little teeth and biting at the air. There was no life in its milky eyes. No breath animated its torn and bloody chest. This was the dark magic of the Others. The promise had been for the absence of death but this certainly was not life. Yagga saw it then too and dropped the writhing creature to the dirt floor. She picked up the black-bladed knife and drove it through the little girl's eye socket. She lay still then.

"What have I done?" said Yagga almost to herself. She handed Flira the knife.

"What do I do with this?" she asked.

"You take it and you run" Yagga said flatly.

Outside was chaos. Those they had lost had certainly come back to them but not as they had been. They saw a man pleading with his wife to stop biting him and that he was sorry for thinking she had died. The obviously dead women bore him to the ground and continued to tear him apart. Pools of blood glinted blackly in the moonlight. They watched as Flira's own father staggered his way between the huts. He had been dead for days and seeing him again ripped her heart open once more. Yagga put a staying hand on her arm and pulled her out of sight.

"We must get my sister. She's all alone, "pleaded Flira. The hut was near and the two crept through the darkness towards it. Her sister's man and their son had been lost to the sickness. She prayed that she would indeed find her sister alone.

Suddenly, a nude man with grave dirt still in his gnashing teeth came lunging out of the darkness toward them. His milky eyes caught the moonlight causing them to shine in the night not unlike the eyes of the Others. He went directly for Flira. She tried to push him back, but she was no match for the large ghoul. Then Yagga was there between her and the hungry dead.

"Get to your sister child! You must save as many as you can. GO!" the older woman yelled to her apprentice.

Flira started forward to help her mentor, but the dead man was tearing her wrinkled, old throat apart before she could take a step. With her very dying breath, Yagga had thought only of her people. She turned away from the bloody scene and continued to creep and dodge her way in the direction of her sister's hut.

She pulled the entrance flap aside and stepped into the darkness. It took Flira's eyes a moment to adjust to the scant light cast by the dying coals in the brazier. She saw her sister sitting in the dark wrapped in furs.

"Sister! We have to leave. It's not safe here," Flira whispered harshly.

"I can't leave. I must feed the baby," her sister said.

Flira reached over and pulled the furs off of her sister. She was holding her little son, now grey with the parlor of death, to her breast. She was smeared with blood, and there was an audible chewing, smacking sound.

"He's not wanted milk in many seasons but now he needs it more than ever. Give me my fur back. My baby is so cold," she said with the merry lilt of someone who's mind has truly broken.

Without thinking, Flira grabbed the creature that was once her nephew and dispatched him with the black blade. Her sister dazedly protested as she wrapped her tightly in furs to staunch the bleeding of her wounds.

"He's sleepy," she heard her sister remark softly at the sight of her now twice dead son laying on the floor. She took her sister firmly by the arm and fled with her into the night.

***

They ran blindly into the darkness, gradually leaving the sounds of carnage behind them. As the sun's first rays crested the horizon and the world began to fill with light, Flira felt they were safe enough to stop and catch their breath. The dawn revealed a nearby stream, and they stopped for a drink and a rest. Flira's sister had been silent through their flight. Flira could only imagine what pain, both physical and mental, she must be experiencing.

She had to help her sister drink. Her eyes were glassy, and she felt clammy and cold.

"Let's get these wounds cleaned up" she said, and her sister only nodded.

Flira unwrapped the furs from her sister's wounds and started to wash them with water from the stream. As the dried, crusted blood was rinsed away, it revealed angry, ragged wounds with red and black streaks radiating out from them. The bites oozed a foul-smelling green pus. How could infection this severe have set in so fast? Her sister, still in a near catatonic daze, seemed unconcerned and did not even flinch when the torn flesh was probed. She redressed the wounds and they both laid down in some soft grass to rest.

Sleep found them both quickly, though Flira's was fitful. She dreamed of teeth that bit and eyes that glowed. She could still hear the gurgling growl of the undead, ringing in her ears. She could hear them still so vividly. No, she could actually hear it! Flira opened her eyes to find herself staring into the glassy orbs of her now dead sister. She tried to scramble away. Her sister caught Flira by the arm and sank her teeth deep into the meat of her forearm. With her other hand, Flira fumbled out the black blade from her belt and drove it up to the handle into her sister's eye. The creature's body went immediately limp and released Flira's arm from its jaws.

She stood up and staggered away, with her hand clamped over the deep bite to stop the bleeding. It felt like cold fire and made her head feel both light and heavy. She knew she had to get as far away from here as she could. She walked through the dizziness and fatigue. There was no way of knowing if the creatures would stay in the village or if they too would venture down from the hills. She had to get as much distance between her and her village as possible.

Seeing that the mountains were behind her, she knew that she was heading east. There was another fairly large village about three days away from her own. Yagga and some of the other villagers would go a few times a year to trade goods and gossip. She knew the medicine woman there was good and could help her with her wound.

So Flira walked. She kept the mountains behind her and walked. She was able to find some late berries and good grasses to sustain her. She grew weak though and had to stop and rest often. There was a fever setting in but she knew it would all be ok if she just made it to the village.

When one evening she finally spotted the glow of fires that signaled she was near, she was unsure how many days it had been. Flira was so tired that she stumbled and fell. What harm would it do if I laid here and rested a moment? She thought. I will catch my breath and then go. By the time she rose and stumbled into the village it was quite late and most of the villagers were sleeping. She did however spot a young man tending a watch fire near the edge of the huts. She shuffled towards him, and he rose to greet her. By the time the light of the fire illuminated her milky eyes and bared teeth, it was too late.

THE HOLLOW

A blade of light cut through the small gap between the curtain and window frame and burned its way onto Luke's sleeping face. The daylight stabbed him in the eye forcing him to acknowledge that day had come and maybe he should start thinking about getting up. Glancing at the clock on the cluttered bedside table he found that it was 10:35 am and he was officially three hours late for work. No point in getting up now. Must have forgotten to set the alarm. What did it matter anyway.

He fished his phone from the pile of candy wrappers and empty Mountain Dew cans that surrounded his bed like a moat. Sure enough, there were several missed calls, texts, and a couple voicemails from Jenna at the office. He let the phone fall from hand back into the sea of detritus on the floor. With a sigh and grumble he pulled the thick comforter over his head and tried to go back to sleep. Today was ruined. He was good at that, Luke thought. How many jobs had he had in just the last year? Something always went wrong. At the sandwich place he lost his temper at some bitch customer. The print shop was so hard. They expected him to carry those giant rolls of paper around like a pack mule. The gas station and the pet store went bad because he was just having a hard time caring enough to go. Same thing with the shoe store and the smoke shop. Now it was happening again with the call center. He should really just face the fact that he's a piece of shit and end it. What good was he doing anyone? His jaw clenched and he squeezed his eyes shut trying to hold back the tears that forced their way through.

He lay like that for over an hour. Curled into a tight ball under the blankets, crying and cycling through every mistake he had ever made and how he had ruined his life. Eventually the tears ebbed, and his bladder ached. Finally, Luke emerged from the nest of his bed, stumbling his way through the empty food wrappers and piles of dirty clothes that covered the floor. His room stunk. He stunk. Luke felt so pathetic. In the bathroom he stared at himself in the mirror. This was never a good idea, but he couldn't help himself. The sallow, blotchy skin and sagging bags under his eyes made him look so much older than his 27 years. He ran a hand down his chin and the scraggly sporadic hairs that were his best attempt at a beard. He couldn't even do that. Every guy he knew could grow a beard but when he tried, he looked like he had mange. On top of being a loser he was also ugly. Worthless. Stupid. An absolute waste of space. There was no point. No reason to continue. In that moment a switch flipped inside him. The sadness and self-hatred reached its apex causing his mind to collapse in on itself. A blank calm came over him. It was not a clear intention or conscious thought that directed him to walk into the kitchen and open the junk drawer. It was as though he was watching someone else's hands take the utility knife out and carry it back to his room. When he sat on the edge of his bed and opened the blade it was a stranger that did these things while Luke simply observed numbly. He did not really feel the knife as it sliced that line down his left wrist. The flesh that it tore was someone else's. He felt no connection to the blood that welled up.

By the time Luke's roommate found him he was barely clinging to life. James called 911 and the paramedics were able to get there in just enough time to save Luke's life.

***

He spent the night in the emergency room while nurses rushed to fill him back up with other people's blood. It seemed he had left most of his own on the bed and floor. They filled him up with blood, plasma, and sedatives. Luke lay there, feeling so entirely empty. When the psychologist came Luke could only blink at her and mumble half-hearted responses. Yes, he had done it on purpose. No, he didn't know why. No, there was no one he wanted to call. Yes, he was sorry. Luke didn't know if that was true though. Was he sorry he did it, or sorry he failed? Though he recognized the cliché, he could not help feeling like even more of a failure for not being able to complete this final task. He also felt like shit that he had put his roommate through this. It had not crossed his mind that James would be the one to deal with the fallout. Luke felt so low.

Luke was informed that he was being held for a mandatory 72 hours for observation. He was told that someone would be in to transfer him to a facility as soon as a bed opened up. In the meantime he lay tied with soft restraints to the gurney in the busy emergency room listlessly staring at the ceiling. Occasionally someone would pull the curtain of his cubicle aside to offer a sip of water or check his vitals. He felt so detached from the situation. Like it was a story he was watching play out and not a terrible and important moment in his own life. The sedatives were probably not helping his disassociated state.

At around 6am a bed opened up at a psychiatric facility in a town nearby. Two orderlies from Pecan River Psychiatric came to collect Luke—a tall, bald man with tattoos and understanding eyes named Todd and a small stout woman who had serious cool aunt energy named Rozz. Though it seemed he had drifted in and out Luke didn't think he had gotten any actual sleep. He was so groggy while the two orderlies were getting his transfer papers filled out. They gave Luke some clean sweatpants, a t-shirt, and a pair of shower shoes to wear and helped him change out of his hospital gown.

He wasn't combative or argumentative. He didn't care. He felt so empty, so exhausted with everything. It was like everything that made Luke "Luke" had been cored out of him and he was just a husk going through the motions. He was a tin man automaton.

***

The next couple days were a blur of sameness. Luke called his roommate and thanked him. He wasn't going to kick Luke out at least. James was a good dude.

Luke went to group and took the pills that they gave him. He was polite and compliant. He went through all the motions they wanted him to. All the while knowing deep down that once he got back home, he would try again to end it. Not that he was planning to or that he even really wanted to but he simply knew he would. It felt inexorable. He was caught in the flowing path of predestination, and he didn't really give a shit. He had no real thoughts in his head. No real emotions in his chest. All he could feel was his own emptiness.

On the second morning when he swallowed his pills at the nurses' station, he heard a 'plunk'. He *HEARD* them rattle down his gullet and hit the bottom of his stomach. It was like listening to a pebble getting thrown down a deep well. He froze, eyes wide. Was he having audio hallucinations now?

"You ok honey?" The nurse asked from behind the plexiglass window of the nurses' station.

"Yeah. Um, I'm fine. Yeah."

Luke gave his head a shake and staggered back to his room. Trying not to look too obvious, he walked briskly to his room; jogging the last corridor when no one was looking. Rushing into his room he closed the door behind him and went directly to the small scratched up shatter proof mirror that was screwed to the wall. He opened his mouth wide and tried to look down his own throat. Instead of the usual fleshy pink that one would expect to see, there was a hole. It was just darkness suggesting a great chasm. He couldn't quite tell what he was looking at. If only he had a flashlight or a phone to get a better look. He had felt so hollow. Was it turning into a deeper delusion? He had heard of a condition where sufferers believed that they had died and were now a rotting animated corpse. Was he experiencing something like that? Had he tipped fully into psychosis? As much as he tried to ignore it, Luke was constantly conscious of the hollowness. When he ate, when he drank, when he took his pills, he could hear the echoing hollow within him. He couldn't ask for help. No one could know. If he said something or asked a nurse for help, they would never let him out of here. He would just have to deal with it until he got home.

After three days of saying what they wanted him to say and doing what they told him to do, he was allowed to go home. James came to pick him up and take him back to their apartment.

"I had to throw out your mattress and your rug. They were pretty gross man. I set up the air mattress in there for though until you can get another bed, " James said quietly as they walked through the apartment door. Sure enough, James had cleaned up. Not just the mattress and throw rug. James had picked up the empty soda bottles and taken out the trash. He had done Luke's laundry and cleaned his bathroom. The air mattress was set up with fresh sheets and blankets. James was such a good roommate. Such a good friend. Luke was stunned. He paused in the bedroom doorway.

"Thank..thank you so much," his voice trembled, on the verge of tears.

James put a hand on Luke's shoulder. "It's ok man. I thought you might feel better coming home to a clean room."

Luke felt something stir in him. Down in his stomach. A flutter. A slight warmth.

"Thanks man," Luke mumbled distracted now by this new sensation. "I, um. I'm gonna lay down for a bit."

"Yea dude. Get some rest. Let me know if you wanna grab some food or something, "James said back as Luke closed the bedroom door.

His phone was charging on the bedside table. James really had thought of everything. He picked it up and walked into the bathroom. He turned on the overhead light as well as the bright vanity lights. First, he stood in front of the mirror and opened his mouth wide. He could see the dark cavern at the back of his throat but nothing else. He felt the flutter again. A shifting like something was moving. It wasn't a gurgle or spasm. No, this was no normal stomach sensation. It felt like there was something in there. Something alive. In his mind's eye he could see a ball of writhing slugs or a coiled snake. Surly whatever lived inside him was dark and vile.

With trembling hands Luke turned on the video camera and the flashlight functions of his phone. He hit record and pointed it down his gullet. As soon as he pointed the little flashlight of the phone down his throat, whatever was down there started thrashing frantically. Then a sound came. It was high pitched and echoed up from the depths of the hollow. Several agitated exclamations erupted from the thrashing, writhing thing within him. His hands were shaking so badly that he had to try multiple times to get the playback working to see the video he just took. Squinting down at the screen, holding it practically to his nose, he struggled to make sense of what he was seeing. He zoomed in. Staring up at the camera with big blinking eyes was a chirping little baby bird. He watched the clip again and again with a hand instinctively on his stomach. The little bird's wide, black eyes stared pleadingly at the camera. He could hear the muffled chirps and little flutters of its tiny wings. Luke was not empty nor did he harbor some vile, crawling, slithering thing as he had imagined. Instead, it was this defenseless little baby bird.

New worries rushed in. Was it ok? Was it hungry? Should he try to take it out? He had to help it. Protect it.

Luke got on his phone and did some internet searching on bird care. He went to the kitchen and made a bowl of cereal. He read that you can feed baby birds cereal and milk. He took tiny bites at first, thinking only of the food getting to the bird. Soon though Luke was ravenous. How long had it been since he had eaten. His appetite had nearly disappeared over those last few months, but it seemed to be back now with a vengeance. He put the bowl to his face and drank the last bit of milk greedily. As soon as he finished, he was overwhelmed by fear that he might have drowned the poor little bird. He sat still for a moment listening and feeling for movement. There. A flutter. Again, he put his phone camera to his open mouth. The little bird's eyes blinked sleepily his little belly bulging with the meal. Luke also felt full and content.

That afternoon he sat in the living room with James and watched a movie. It was the new action comedy starring a retired wrestler alongside a skinny heartthrob. Luke and James laughed at the funny parts and exclaimed at the action. Neither men could remember the last time they had actually hung out like that. They ordered pizza and played video games. When Luke laughed or got excited, he could feel the bird fluttering happily.

In the morning Luke decided to open his curtains and let the sun shine into his room. He stood in front of the window and opened his mouth wide to try and let the bird get a bit of sun. It started chirping wildly and he could feel its little feet climbing up him from the inside. Was it trying to escape? Instinctively he clamped his mouth shut to prevent it jumping out. It banged its tiny head against Luke's teeth and pecked at Luke's tongue. Slowly Luke opened his mouth. The baby bird sat there on his tongue. Carefully Luke held his phone up with the front-facing camera on. The little bird was sitting contently in Luke's mouth sunning itself. It nestled in and closed its eyes. It looked so at peace. A tear fell from Luke's eye.

After seeing how happy the sun made his baby bird feel, Luke began walking every morning from his apartment to the little park a few blocks away. He sat on a bench in a secluded corner and opened his mouth to let the baby bird enjoy the sun and fresh air. It never ventured farther than his tongue and Luke quickly stopped worrying about it jumping out. It seemed silly now how he had been afraid.

As time went on the bird grew. Luke did everything he could to take care of it. He fed it well and took it out and talked to it. When it ate though so did Luke. While the bird was enjoying the sun on its face, Luke was enjoying it too. By default, he was taking care of himself. Luke found a job at a warehouse. It was hard work but for the first time he felt like he was working toward something. He had purpose.

The bird grew as babies tend to do. Its little pin features became beautiful, thick plumage. It had become a shimmering blue-grey with bright, intelligent eyes. It was big, too. Too big to sit comfortably on Luke's tongue. It could only sit in his throat and peek its little head out of Luke's mouth.

Eventually it did begin to come out to stretch its wings. At first it sat on Luke's shoulder staying close. It perched there, fussing with Luke's hair while they walked or watched movies. A while after that it started flying for short bursts. It flew to the clothes hamper and nestled in. It flew to a low branch of a tree in the park. It sat there a moment and chirped happily at Luke before fluttering back to him. Luke could see how happy the bird was when it explored these small freedoms. It made him happy too. Mostly anyway. There was always a little bite of sadness underneath it. He wasn't sure how he would cope without his little friend.

When the day came that his bird finally flew away and did not return, all Luke could think was how beautiful the sun was on its feathers.

JUNK GUYS USA

"Hello and welcome to Junk Guys USA. I'm your host, Neal, and me and my buddy Dave here are coming to you from beautiful Tennessee. Let's see what treasures we can find."

Neal Kendrick's too white, too wide TV smile dropped from his face as soon as he finished the intro. His handsomely rugged face took on a peevish scowl. He ran long fingers through his perfectly salt-and-pepper hair. His hand came back wet with sweat. He and his business partner Dave Coolidge were out in the oppressive heat of a Tennessee August while their young cameraman, Mitch, filmed them. They were standing next to the iconic blue "Junk Guys USA" van with a beautiful old tobacco barn for a backdrop. Neal pinched the bridge of his nose. The drone of the cicadas was deafening. Would they even be able to use that shot with all the noise? Would they be able to use any of this?

So far Tennessee had been a total bust. Out of the three properties that their team had pre-selected only one of them had really had anything worth a damn and that guy had been one of the most unpleasant people to date. He had agreed and signed the releases days ago but when Neal and Dave showed up he decided he didn't want to sell anything. Or maybe he just thought the shows pockets were deeper than they actually were.

They were three seasons into their show about traveling to rural America and finding diamond-in- the-rough antiques in old barns and hoarder houses. Viewership had been steadily dropping and the money well was about to go dry. He and Dave might be out of the job soon. Neal had gotten an offer a while back to do a different travel show but would that offer still stand now? Dave didn't seem to give a shit. His constant optimism made Neal want to strangle Dave. That fat little neck beard didn't understand what was at stake. Not that Neal had let on how badly in debt he was. Well, how far in debt THEY were. Somewhere between his nasty divorce, too many nights spent at the club, and even more days at the horse track, Neal had needed to dip into the company coffers. It wouldn't have been a big deal if things hadn't started to tank on the show. They were already losing sponsors. Something needed to go right. He couldn't let this trip be wasted.

"What do you say we do a little poking round? It's still early" Dave said.

Usually when they had a busted trip like this, they could head to the general store in some podunk town and ask who had the best junk. Usually, the locals knew right away who to direct them to. Every town out here had a general store where the village busy bodies hung out sipping coffee all day. Those busy bodies could always tell you where to find the local eccentric hoarder that would be happy to show you around and tell stories about their junk. It was always a fine line between beloved eccentric and crazed gun-toting hillbilly though. That's why they usually had a scouting team come out ahead of time. Let the interns get screamed at and have guns pulled on them. Cold calling hillbillies was a good way to get the talent killed. These were desperate times though. It was really the only way to salvage this trip.

The three of them climbed back in the van and turned on the AC. The van had only been sitting about ten minutes but was already a sweat box. There was no phone service out here in the sticks, so they pulled out the trusty paper roadmap.

"Looks like there's a tiny shithole about ten miles from here," Mitch said rapping an index finger on the map to indicate the location. "Innsmouth Holler" he added "I don't think we've been through there yet."

"I hope the general store there has a slushy machine. I want to just dunk my head in it," Dave said with a smile as sweat ran down his forehead.

The town was well off the main road. The blacktop leading into town was so beat up that it was more like a gravel road. Neal bet the county road crews hadn't been here since Hoover was in charge. They passed the occasional tarpaper shack or sagging single-wide trailer. Old farmhouses dotted the landscape as well. Broken windows like empty eye sockets seemed to watch them as they drove by. All the structures seemed to be long abandoned. Had this once been a more populous area? As they went on the trees and bushes got closer into the road. In places it was so overgrown that branches scraped the sides of the van as it bounced from one pothole to another.

This part of the country was so depressing. Everywhere you looked you could see the steady decline of the local economy. The corporations that came in promising prosperity just to take all the coal or lumber they could and disappear, leaving the citizens with empty pockets and cancer in their lungs. This was also the type of place though where you were just as likely to find a forgotten '57 Chevy in perfect condition hiding under a tarp in an old barn. The best antiques always came from the saddest places.

They passed the town limit sign with its stereotypical bullet holes.

"Population 300, huh?" Mitch exclaimed "talk about a small town."

"Hopefully it's still here" Neal worried "look at this road! It's so overgrown and the paving is almost gone."

The trees soon opened up and they could see a couple buildings. On the right side of the road was the obligingly general store. This one even sported gas pumps and a mechanic garage. On the left a tiny post office building leaned drunkenly to one side. The window glass was missing, and the front door yawned open into darkness. It had obviously been unused for some time. Next to that a large barn hulked. On the front was a faded "feed and seed" sign. A handful of other building stood rotting on their foundations, suggesting that this may have once been a small but thriving main street. Neal noticed a large tree growing through the roof of one building and judged the towns heyday must have been some time ago.

With lit neon signs and handful of beat-up pickup trucks in the lot, the general store told them that it was indeed open for business.

The three men stepped out of the van and into the sweltering afternoon heat. They opened the ragged screen door and stepped inside a time capsule. The space was dim and full of shadows. It took a moment for their eyes to adjust to the gloom after being in the too bright summer sun. A large central fan spun lazily over a bare wood lunch counter where an elderly couple sat. The man was stout and in the obligatory overalls while the woman was rail thin sporting a sun dress that hung off of her like a scarecrow done up for Sunday brunch. A man in a long sleeve button up shirt stood behind the counter organizing a display of cigarettes. There was an old man sitting on a stool in a shadowy corner whittling a stick who looked like something out of central casting. Cobwebs fluttered from the antlers of moth-eaten deer heads mounted along the walls. A banner advertising Moxie soda sagged behind the counter. Everything looked covered in a century of dust, including the people. There was no slushy machine. All conversation stopped when the three obvious city folk walked in. The wide set watery eyes of the shopkeeper fixed on Neal with immediate disdain.

"Kin I halp ye?" he drawled. As he did, a little runnel of brown liquid leaked from his mouth.

Neal couldn't keep the slight wince from his face as he hoped the liquid was tobacco juice. Recovering his composure Neal mustered his best friendly smile and went into his spiel about the show and what they were looking for. The storekeeper and the two at the counter stared at him in silence until he was done and then a beat more. The old man in the corner never raised his head from his whittling.

"Yeah, there's a spot. On down to the Marsh place. Granny Marsh got all sorts down there," the shopkeeper said finally.

He agreed to draw a map and explained in detail how to get there. The others sat in silence. Neal wondered to himself if these people were related. They all seemed to have the same wide set eyes, wide sunken mouth and thin lips. Frankly they creeped him out. He glanced at the old man in the corner again. He still had his head down. What was that on his neck? In the gloom Neal thought he saw some kind of cuts or folds on the old man's neck. What the hell was he looking at? He found himself staring at the old man, but Mitch had the directions in his hand

117

and was calling out for them to go. Probably just a trick of the dim lighting Neal decided and followed Mitch and Dave out to the van.

"We aren't really going, are we?" Dave asked. "I mean, those people were creepy as shit, right?"

"It'll be fine. We'll go say howdy to Granny Marsh and if it's no good then we'll leave. Call Claire at the office and let her know where we are if that will make you feel better," Mitch said.

Dave checked his phone. "I still don't have any reception. What about you guys?" No one had reception.

"Let's just get out there and get this over with. Besides, it's always the sketchy places that turn out be gold mines," said Neal.

The men drove down the narrow road following the directions the shopkeeper had given them.

Before long they were pulling into the driveway marked with a blue milk jug as described by the man in the store. The long driveway was lined on either side by rusted out cars and trucks. There seemed to be vehicles of every type spanning the last several decades. An ancient, rusted Ford pickup from the

'40s sat bumper to bumper with a faded '90s Honda hatchback. Grass grew up through the bumpers and vines snaked around rusted frames.

Finally, they came to a dilapidated two-story farmhouse with a large barn and several smaller outbuildings. Witchgrass and weeds grew high all around the whole property. There was slat-ribbed old white horse picking idly at the weeds in front of the wide front porch. The horse was so thin that it was more anatomical study of bone structure than beast. It looked filthy too. Dirt and filth coated its body and ran down its back side. Was it sick? It reminded Neal of a painting from the renaissance he had seen. It had been of death riding a pale horse. The horse looked like this one. Despite the heat, Neal shivered.

They parked the van and Mitch jumped out with his camera to get some establishing shots. He filmed from the yard while Neal and Dave walked onto the rickety porch and knocked. When they got close, they could smell the hoarder stink. Smelled like a cat lady house. They had been in plenty of those. He knew it would be bad when he could smell the cats from outside, and this one smelled especially rank.

To their surprise a little girl answered the door. She couldn't have been more than five and was as dirty and thin as the horse out front. She just blinked up at them with the same too big, too wet eyes as the people from the store. Was that an inbreeding thing? Was everyone in this town related? In a town this small both things were probably true.

"We're looking for Granny Marsh, sweetie. Is she here? Is there a grownup we can talk to?" Dave leaned down and asked.

She stared and blinked slowly. Suddenly the tiny girl opened her mouth wider than it seemed possible and let out a deafening screech. It was shocking and ear-piercing. She then darted off into the deep shadows of the house, leaving the door wide open and then men stunned into silence.

"What the actual fuck was that?" Mitch finally said.

"Hillbilly shenanigans I guess," said Neal. "Might as well go in and see if anyone is home."

They stepped through the doorway into the gloomy foul-smelling house. Neal had expected to be greeted by a herd of cats. Judging by the smell there must be hundreds. None came though. Nor did he see the telltale piles of droppings or clumps of fur. Instead, it was mostly old furniture and moldering cardboard boxes.

"Hello! Is anyone there? Little girl? We are looking for Granny Marsh! Is anyone there?" Dave bellowed into the gloom. The floorboards groaned beneath their feet.

"What the hell you think yer do'n?" came a furious voice from behind them on the porch.

The men stopped and turned back to the still open front door they had just come through. The figure was backlit, so it was hard to make out the features, but it seemed to be a young man maybe early teens and another very small child. Neal immediately put on his 1000-watt smile and went into salesman mode.

"I'm so sorry. We hadn't meant to intrude. There was a little girl. She let us in then ran away. I'm Neal from the show 'Junk Guys USA'. We were hoping to talk to Granny Marsh about possibly filming an episode," he said, walking towards the young man and extending his hand for a shake. "

Did you say TV?" The young man's demeanor changed abruptly from angry and defensive to friendly and eager.

"That's right son. We want to put you and your family on the TV. First though we need to talk to Granny or whatever adult is in charge here."

The young man shook Neal's hand. It was everything he had for Neal not to immediately recoil when the kid's filthy hand shook his own. Every finger had black filth caked beneath the nails and open sores oozed in several places. They stepped back out into the relative light of the porch, and they could see that this child also bore the too large eyes and wide mouth that seemed to be the trademark look of Innsmouth Holler.

"I'm Billie and this is little baby Arlene" he said, gesturing to the toddler that was now clinging to his leg.

Mitch jumped back and cried out "what the fuck?" when he shifted the camera down, getting his first good look at the small child.

"Dude shut up," Dave snapped back, though he himself had very nearly had the same reaction.

Little baby Arlene not only had the wide set eyes and frog mouth but also sported a severely cleft pallet that gave the impression that her face was in the process of splitting in two. The cleft was so severe that it left the little girl wholly without a nose. Instead, there was a wet, meaty fissure that ran from her mouth to her brow line, oozing puss and mucus. Her sinuses were exposed and clearly infected. Thin wisps of hair clung to her head like cobwebs. This little girl was clearly in need of medical attention. Dave felt heartsick for her. They had a job to do though. They could call Child Protective Services once they got back to the hotel.

The young man seemed completely oblivious to their reactions to the toddler.

"Granny is down in the barn. She gonna be so happy. We ain't had no visitors is a long while and you all being tv people, well she's liable to have a fit," Billie said, turning and starting to walk in the direction of the sagging barn.

"Where are your parents?" Neal asked.

"Oh, they all out hunting ginseng up on the mountain" he responded. "I'm in charge up here now since I'm the oldest. Gotta make sure granny gets fed and warshed up. The little'uns, too. Gotta make sure they all do'n right.".

He rambled on like that as they closed the yard to the barn. "

How many of you kids are there?" Dave asked.

"I'm not righty sure sir. Everyone sends they little'uns here to sit at Granny's knee. Maybe 10? 15? Gets hard to keep track."

"We should just go man. This place gives me the creeps bad," Mitch whispered hoarsely to Neal.

"Don't be such a pussy. Keep filming. We have to see what they have and pull an episode out of this shitshow," Neal spat back.

Mitch followed Neal, Dave, and the two youngsters sheepishly into the gloom of the barn. It was even hotter inside the barn than outside. The air was thick with heat and humidity. Neal could hear the little girls gurgling breaths wheezing wetly through her open sinuses as she toddled along beside the older child.

The barn was packed full of junk just as they had supposed it would be. Old bicycles, oil cans, and milk crates jostled with tires and moldering hay. Dave immediately spotted a giant enamel sign from a defunct gas station chain.

"Oh man, this thing is in amazing shape" he cried out gleefully as he started to pull it from the debris.

Neal soon spotted a dirty but in good shape 1942 Indian Motorcycle. They spotted treasure after treasure as they walked through. As they worked, they were joined by more children. Pale and big-eyed they followed the men around. Two became five, five became eight. They seemed to range in age from toddler to preteen. While all of them sported the distinctive local look of large eyes and wide mouths, many also exhibited additional deformities. A couple had cleft palates of varying degrees and one had the flippered hands of polydactyly. The men tried hard not to stare at the children though it was difficult. The children followed them silently, watching their every move with rapt attention. It made the three men more than a bit uncomfortable.

"Where did you say your Granny was? We'd love to start making some offers on this stuff" Dave asked the young man.

"She's working down in the canning cellar. We got some nice treasures down there too if'n ye wanna see," Billie responded, gesturing to a door near the back of the barn.

They followed Billie through the old wooden door with the procession of children following behind like a tragic little parade. They walked down a short flight of steps to a low-ceilinged, earthen-floored room lined with shelves and packed with junk. Dimly flickering fluorescent bulbs cast a weak light. The cool air down here smelled foul. Though it was a relief from the sweltering heat, Neal would have preferred the relatively fresh air of the barn above.

While the three men glanced around taking in the space, antique hunting was now far from their minds. Their eyes adjusted to the dark shadows in the building. Then the men spotted them. Hiding amongst the junk were faces. Tiny grotesque faces dotted the piles. The men stopped, taken aback. Their eyes went wide and mouths slack as the small, twisted frames started shuffling out surrounding them. They were all shapes and sizes, though many were so deformed it was hard to guess any specifics of age or gender. Some had limbs that were missing or fused while others sported extra appendages. There were some whose eyes were the opaque, milky white of cave-dwelling fish. Some were so bent and twisted by deformity that the mind boggled at how they could still be a living creature. There were dozens of them. Every horror imaginable and unimaginable was represented in this grotesque horde. The only unified features were the large wide set eyes and too wide mouth. They surrounded the men. The dim flickering light giving them a distinctly malevolent cast. Mitch swung his camera around wildly, trying to film this horror.

The men didn't realize that they had started screaming until Billie yelled, "Quit yer squall'n. You gonna disturb the babies."

. He was now pointing a shotgun in their faces. He must have grabbed it from somewhere while they had been distracted by the other children.

"Fuck this" Mitch declared as he threw up his hands and turned toward the steps leading back up.

"You stop right there buster" Billie called.

Mitch didn't listen and kept walking. The shotgun blast was deafening at such close range. The cameraman was knocked violently forward and onto the ground, the back of his head a gory pit. There was no question that he was quite dead. The crotch of Dave's jeans went dark with urine as terror made his bladder release. Then to pile horror upon horror, the monstrous children began to swarm the corpse. Dave and Neal quickly looked away, but the wet slurping, squishing noises told them enough.

Dave put his arms up in a gesture of surrender. Neal picked up the now blood-spattered camera and kept filming though his hands were violently shaking. This was so very, very far outside of their reality. They heard the door above them slam shut and a lock clicking into place.

"What do you want?" Dave sobbed.

"I want you to come meet Granny," Billie gestured with the shotgun into the gloom of the storeroom.

"There's a door up there to yer left. Open it an' walk on down. Imma be right here behind you so mind yerself ."

Though they didn't want to go, they had no desire to stand there listening to their coworker being sloppily eaten by a hoard of deformed children. In about twenty feet they came to the back of the room and the door on the left. Dave was in the lead, and he opened it. A stench like cat piss and death rolled out, making Dave hesitate until he felt Billie nudge him with the barrels of the shotgun. There were steps leading down. They walked down and down. It was dark and they navigated using the light on the front of the camera. The walls went from wood to earth to damp weeping stone. The rough wooden stairs transitioned into carved stone steps. Every hesitation was met with a nudge from Billie's shotgun. As they went deeper, they started to hear sounds rising from the deep darkness. There was a clicking scraping sound accompanied by a deep groan or grumble that echoed through the stone. Eventually the wall to their right dropped away and they saw that they were walking down the side of an immense natural cavern. The terrible smell intensified as they descended. At least it was cooler down here. Now the men were pouring sweat from fear and not the summer heat.

"I'm so sorry, Dave" Neal said sorrowfully. "This is all my fault. We wouldn't be here if I hadn't pushed it. I got greedy, man. I'm so sorry for everything" he said, as he started to cry softly. Dave said nothing. It was all he had to keep putting one foot in front of the other.

After what seemed like several eternities, they finally reached the bottom. A few more steps took them to a natural stone corridor lit by flicking tallow candles. The soft light danced across flowing twisting petroglyphs. Shapes that hurt your eyes to look at too closely. What on earth was this place?

"Are you still filming? "Dave whispered to Neal.

"Yeah. No one would believe us if I didn't "he replied.

After a couple twists and turns, the tunnel opened up into a grand space. The ceiling stretched up into darkness and the walls could have held a football field. In the center like some great regal slug sat a monster. The children they had seen were at least monstrous in a humanoid way. In a way they could wrap their minds around. This was something entirely OTHER. It filled the space with its slimy oozing girth. Pulpy and wet, a broad round head reared up from a tubular body. Spindly clawed appendages clacked and flailed down both sides of its mass. It's eyes were immense white orbs set wide on the thing's head and seemed to glow with an inner malevolent light. Great gobs of slime ran freely from the corners of a wide yawning mouth filled with rows upon rows of needle teeth.

Neal dropped his camera to the floor as his body went limp with terror.

"NO! No, no, no, no, no, no," Dave yammered, unable to fit this into any model of a familiar reality. The two men knew then for sure that they would not live to see another sunrise.

"Meet Granny, fellas. She'd love y'all to stay for supper."

HER HOUSE

Ruby couldn't help but smile as she placed the last of the figurines on the shelf. She arranged them just so. The figurines had once belonged to Ruby's grandmother, and Ruby knew her grandmother would have been delighted to see her prized miniatures on display and loved, just as they had been when she was still alive. This was her nice thing. The tiny perfect figurines sitting neatly on the polished cherry wood shelves made her feel at peace. Looking at them made her think of her grandmother and how proud she would have been of Ruby. Sometimes it was so hard to keep it together. To keep pushing forward. But looking at those precious little bits of porcelain, she could almost feel her grandmother's reassuring arm on her shoulder.

As she stepped back to survey her work, a peace washed over her. Now this was truly HER home. Sure, she had moved out of her parent's place over a year ago, but living in a house with five roommates isn't exactly being "on your own." In a house with no privacy, nothing ever feels like it's yours. The constant squabbles and weeknight partying hardly felt like what she thought being an adult would be. This, on the other hand —

sitting on her brand-new thrift shop sofa, sipping tea and enjoying a comfortable silence with her orderly little living room . . . this was actual adulthood. Feeling particularly mature, she set her tea mug down on a coaster on her battered, curb-find coffee table and went to make lunch.

After a couple days, the relief and novelty of having a house to herself was starting wear off. The nighttime was the worst. When you are in a dark, silent house, your mind begins to fill in the emptiness. Every shadow becomes a hulking fiend. Every creak and groan of the house is a serial killer secretly living in your attic, just waiting for the right moment to come down and kill you. Every possible worst-case scenario runs through your head at the slightest breeze in the trees outside the window. It made her feel like a child again, terrified of what could be lurking under the bed. This decidedly did not make her feel much like the strong independent woman she wanted to be. She tried playing on her phone or watching television, but that certainly wasn't helping her get any sleep. Morning would still come early, and she needed every ounce of rest she could get to be ready for work. No matter what, she could not shake the sense of being watched.

One morning, about two weeks after moving in, as she was standing in her kitchen sipping her coffee and trying to shake off her drowsiness, Ruby noticed something. There, on the shelf of figurines. She stared at the shelf a full minute, trying to figure out what was different. A miniature rabbit with big, cartoonish eyes, holding the most delicately sculpted bouquet of flowers, was facing the wrong direction and was precariously close to the edge of the shelf. She walked over and straightened it. How on earth had that happened? Ruby remembered looking at her little curio shelf last night, as she often did. When she would get home from working a double and feeling like she could not go on, she would stand and look at the figurines, and they never failed to make her smile. This little ritual always gave her that little extra bit of energy and inspiration needed to toil the rest of the night away in front of her computer, working at her online classes.

She couldn't imagine how that figure could have gotten out of place. Considering that no one else had been there, it did not really bear thinking about. She decided to push it out of her mind and go about her day. She didn't have time to freak out over a shifted bit of curio.

That night, Ruby fought through fatigue as she sat at her computer, working on a paper that was due the day before. She stopped to rub her eyes. As she leaned back, something caught her attention in the reflection on her screen. It took a moment for her eyes to focus on it and another long moment for her to process and register what she was seeing. Was that a silhouette of a person in the doorway behind her? Ruby spun around to confront the intruder, only to be met by an empty doorway. Again, it took a beat for her to process what she was experiencing. The lack of sleep was causing her brain to run more slowly. She stared at the unoccupied space, half-expecting the menacing shape to reappear. Nothing—she must have imagined it. Now that the moment was passed, she could no longer trust the memory. Even though it was only seconds ago, she was already talking herself into believing she had merely misinterpreted the combinations of glare and shadows on the screen. Living alone, coupled with the lack of sleep, was making her crazy and paranoid. That was somehow a more comforting thought than the idea that she might have just had a supernatural experience. Taking this as a sign that she was past due to go to bed, she did just that. Luckily, Ruby's fatigue was strong enough to push away any other thoughts of shadow men, allowing her to sleep soundly.

In the morning she found it nearly impossible to haul herself out of bed. She knew she slept through the night, but it felt as though she hadn't gotten any rest at all. The crazy hours must have been catching up to her. She had heard once about the notion of "sleep debt." The idea was that you need a certain amount of rest and sleep, and if you don't get enough, it adds up and accrues interest. This means that one night of good sleep won't do much against a large sleep debt but rather that you need to sleep for longer than the recommended eight hours to start chipping away at the deficit. Like taking a day to sleep in until noon and not change out of your pajamas. Was that the "self-care" thing everyone is always talking about? She wasn't sure about the science behind the theory, but her body was telling her that there might be something to it.

A bleary-eyed Ruby fumbled through making coffee and buttering toast. As she was walking to the living room area to have her breakfast on the couch, she heard something crunch under her slippered foot. As she looked down, she had to make a conscious effort not to drop her coffee mug in shock. On the floor next to her foot, a single, wide eye stared back up at her. She recognized the fragment with its button nose and large pointed ear. The eternally hopeful face of the Finneas Fox figurine lay shattered on the floor. There over by the chair was his finely crafted tail. When she lifted her foot, she saw a tiny delicate black paw among a scattering of unrecognizable debris.

Horror and grief filled her. How could this have happened? Her fatigue-addled mind conjured fourth some deranged maniac who breaks into people's homes for the sole purpose of smashing precious objects and getting off on the small-scale destruction. She took a steadying breath, set her coffee and toast back on the counter and grabbed the hand brush and dustpan. She carefully swept up all the tiny pieces and put them in a little Ziplock bag. She would get some glue on the way home tonight and see if little Finneas could be salvaged. She would deal with this like a practical adult and not a scared, lonely, tired child. Then she thought of the figure in the reflection last night. She shook her head, hoping to physically dislodge the thought. It was too much to unpack this early in the morning. She slurped down her coffee, shoved the toast in her mouth and finished getting ready for work.

Ruby resolved that, when she got home after work, she would be aggressively lazy. It was Friday, and she had no other obligations for the weekend. Maybe she would pay a bit down on that sleep debt. When she came in the door that evening, she saw the bag on the counter containing what was left of her grandmother's fox figurine. She had forgotten the glue. Finneas could wait until tomorrow, though. Tonight, was for trash TV and snacks, anyway.

Ruby took off her shoes and padded into her bedroom to change into some soft pajamas. She didn't bother turning on the bedroom light. By now it was familiar, and enough ambient light was coming in from the kitchen for her to make her way about. She went to her dresser and opened the top drawer, where her pajamas were. As she lifted them out, she saw something in the large mirror attached to the dresser. The PJs fell back into the drawer as her hands went limp with shock. She could feel her eyes widening to their limit and her mouth forming an "O" of surprise. This time there was no mistake. There was a figure in her door. It was tall and distinctly masculine. She was able to break her body out of its paralysis and turn towards the door. Nothing. It was just empty air. No menacing intruder. Just the short hall to the kitchen. She looked back at the mirror, and there it was. The figure seemed to shiver or shimmer with darkness. It made her feel cold in a way that wasn't physical. This was wrong. This being went against all the rules of physics and science. It hurt her to look at it. It was oppressive.

Ruby began to sink down toward the floor. She realized then that she was crying. Why was this happening? What did it want from her? She turned her head back toward the door. This time the figure was there. It was actually there in the room with her. The terror became like a weight, pressing her down into a cower. As she sunk lower to the floor, the figure seemed to grow. It was fully in the room now, looming tall and vicious above her. Tears streamed down her face. Is this how she would die?

The figure raised arms made of shadow, and she heard a crash from the front of the house. The curios! He was the one who killed Finneas! A little seed of rage began to grow in her stomach.

"Stop," she whimpered. There was a sound like rasping whispers, then another tiny crashing sound.

"I said STOP!"

Ruby found herself back on her feet. The little seed in her belly was sprouting into a full-on rage bush. Another crash. The rasping whisper came again, and she recognized it for what it was: a laugh. This creepy motherfucker was laughing at her! He was breaking her grandmother's precious figurines and fucking laughing about it! Her hands clenched into fists, and her back went straight. Taking a step forward, she screamed, "I said fucking stop, you ethereal piece of shit!"

Did the apparition seem to shrink back? Ruby suddenly felt powerful. She took another step forward and stuck a finger into the shadow's face as she continued to give it a piece of her mind.

"Who do you think you are, you creepy bitch?! I don't give a fuck if you died here or if you're some demon shit that thinks it can come harass me! This is MY house! I pay the rent, and I scrub the toilet, and you need to fuck right off! Smashing my gramma's figurines like an angry fucking baby! Get a hobby, you tired ass demonic fuck!" Rudy continued, walking forward, backing the entity toward the door.

As she railed and berated, the entity began to visibly shrink. Its posture changed from tall and looming to hunched and defensive. Then a great gust of wind came through the house. Ruby kept yelling at the thing. The wind carried her words into and through the shadow. It bucked and writhed as though hit by arrows. It began to break apart and then dissolved like dust in the wind.

"That's right, Douche bag the Unfriendly Ghost! You better fucking run! If I see you again, I'mma get some sage and beat your fucking ass with it!" With these words, the last bits of shadow dissipated into the bright light of the kitchen.

Purposefully not looking at the freshly broken figurines as she passed, Ruby walked to the sofa and collapsed in a heap. She pulled an old afghan over herself and reached for the remote control. She felt oddly good. She felt peaceful and powerful. As she put on her favorite British baking show, she thought about words and intentions. She wondered if when a priest or shaman banished a spirit, was it the actual invocation that mattered, or was the power in the intention behind the invocation? Was it just strength of will or character that gives them power? Gramma had always said Ruby was strong and willful.

Ruby smiled to herself, knowing that she wouldn't need to worry about asshole shadows again.

OF MEN AND MICE

The sun was beginning to rise over a quaint middle-class neighborhood in the northeastern US. The one- and two-story single-family homes sat on large lots and were widely spaced. Many of the tidy yards sported flag poles and had big, gas-guzzling trucks and SUVs parked in the driveway. Bret McMillan sat in the kitchen of one such house. He sipped his coffee and watched the dawn light illuminate the "don't tread on me" flag that flapped on his flagpole. He had already been up for over an hour. It didn't matter to him that it was Saturday, and he didn't have to go in for work today. It gave him a certain sense of pride and accomplishment to be up and active before everyone else. He prided himself on being not only ready and prepared for the day, but for life in general.

He took out his phone and started scrolling social media. He listened to a person in a video rail on about celebrity satanists, poisoned vaccines, and the hidden gay agenda. He didn't bother doing an internet search to check any of the "facts" the video spewed. Bret knew that internet search engines and mainstream media twisted the truth or just outright lied. Much better to get his information from independent sources like this.

The neighborhood was starting to wake up now. The golden sunlight was making the dew on the lawns sparkle. He saw his neighbor Chris walking his dog. It was one of those fruity new breeds like Labradoodle or some shit. Bret liked "real" dogs like German shepherds or Doberman pinchers. He didn't have any pets but if he did it would be something badass like that.

His neighborhood was changing, and he didn't much care for it. It had always been a decent middle-class neighborhood full of families and working stiffs. These days though rich out of towners were buying up all the decent houses and making the real estate market go insane. Bret's property tax was going up so drastically that he wasn't sure if he could keep paying if it kept rising. He was from this town; born and bred. The house he had grown up in was just a few blocks away. A lesbian couple owned it now. With house prices like they were, it seemed like everyone was selling. His best friend since elementary school had lived a couple doors down from him. They would help each other with house projects and have cook outs all the time. The two of them had converted Bret's old canning cellar into a full-on survival bunker. They had had such a good time pounding beers and listening to music down there. He was gone now too though. Sold his house for a mint and him and the wife flew off to Florida. Bret still kept up with his old friend through social media, but it wasn't the same. Scrolling through all the pictures of his friend smiling at the beach and going marlin fishing made him sick. Who did he think he was? And the guy that bought the house? Bret's new neighbor? Liberal arts professor from California. His name was Kevin, and he had a cat. What kind of a man has a cat?! No, Bret was not happy with the direction the neighborhood was taking.

The soft ding of his perimeter alarm went off. He stepped over to the small console screen in the hall. His neighbor Stephanie was walking up to his door. She was looking real good today in her tight little running outfit. She must have been going hard this morning. He could see the sweat glistening on her neck and chest. Had she finally decided to leave that cuck husband of hers and find out what it was like to be with a real man? Several salacious scenarios ran through his head. She rang the doorbell, and he walked over to the front of the house to answer her. He opened the door with his best seductive smile.

"Good morning, Stephanie" Bret said as he leaned casually against the doorframe and took a sip of coffee. His eyes followed a bead of sweat as it lazily rolled down from her clavicle and into the cleft of her breasts. His smile broadened. "What can I do for you?" he asked, putting an odd emphasis on the 'do'.

***

Stephanie was mortified by his attention. She always tried to give her neighbor Bret a wide berth. She would never have come here if Crystal hadn't asked her to. Crystal had the job of collecting donations for the annual neighborhood food drive. It was widely known that Bret was a bit of a prepper. The thought was that if he had a bunch of nonperishable food and supplies laying around, that he might be willing to donate some of his older inventory. The community center was really running short right now and needed every can of green beans or box of macaroni they could get. It had been agreed in the community group that she had the best chance of getting this asshole to

144

donate. Standing there now she deeply regretted letting them talk her into this. She knew that he watched her jog most mornings. She would see him leering out of his kitchen window. Lately she had been taking a different route to avoid going past his house. He creeped her out so bad. Now she was face to face with him. He was close enough that she could smell his rotten coffee breath.

Stephanie sighed.

"Hey, Bret. We're doing the annual community food drive. Would you like to contribute? If you have any dry goods laying around, you could donate them" she said.

"I think I might have some stuff in my pantry. You can come in and help me look" he said with a wolffish grin.

Stephanie tried and failed to suppress her disgust. "No. You can just put anything you have in a box and leave it on your porch tomorrow morning. That's when we are doing pickups" she said, starting to back away. Bret noticed her recoiling away from him and his smile dropped.

"I don't know why you try to help those people. If you really want to help them, you should just let them starve. See how fast they get a job then! I worked hard for what I have, and they have no excuse. You people are just making things worse. I changed my mind. I'm not donating shit" he growled.

By now Stephanie was halfway to the sidewalk. She was done. Fuck this guy. This was so not worth it. "Ok, bye" she said curtly as she turned and started jogging back to her house. She tried not to think about how things would have gone if she had gone inside to "look at his pantry." She decided that in the future she would avoid that guy at all costs.

***

"What a bitch" Bret thought.

She was just looking for a handout like the rest of them. It's a dog-eat-dog world out there and only the strong survive. He wasn't about to give what he had worked hard for to some lazy stranger.

As he was walking back into the house his phone started making this loud god-awful bleating siren sound that he had never heard before. He took it out of his pocket and looked at the

146

screen. Instead of seeing the picture of the American flag Punisher skull he had as his lock screen, the words "Special Emergency. Take immediate shelter. Select for details "filled the screen. He had never seen anything like this before. It kind of reminded him of when an Amber Alert came through. This was different though. Cold trepidation filled him. When he hit the "Select for details" button his finger trembled just so. What he read next made his knees go a bit weak and he had to sit down. He flopped down on the sofa and tried to process what he was reading. The text read "SPECIAL ALERT. TAKE IMMEDIATE SHELTER. From the office of the Commander and Chief and Secretary of Defense. We have confirmation of multiple North Korean missiles with nuclear capabilities have been launched at the United States. It is estimated that they will make landfall in the Northeastern US within one hour. Shockwaves and fallout can impact areas far beyond the initial site of landfall. Take shelter underground when possible. More information will follow after impact."

He had been preparing for exactly this. He had a bunker full of supplies. He had a state-of-the-art surveillance and security system. He had solar power battery cells. He had guns and ammo to spare. Now was his time to shine.

He ran down his mental check list and headed into the bedroom to grab clothes. He picked up a laundry basket and started filling it up. He also took it into the kitchen and tossed some bananas and a bag of chips in. He walked around grabbing odds and ends he thought he might like to have down in the bunker. He added the book he had been reading about WWII tanks, his toothbrush, his 9mm pistol, and of course his favorite hat and rifle. Once he felt he had all the things he might need he went outside and headed for the cellar doors on the back of the house that led to the bunker.

Instead of the standard, rather flimsy cellar double doors, the bunker had a single heavy steel door with a keypad and custom locking mechanism. It had been specially made and was supposed to be nearly impenetrable.

Bret keyed in his code and opened the door. As he bent to pick up the laundry basket, he saw one of his neighbors running over.

"What the actual fuck" he exclaimed to himself.

He glanced at his phone. Only 20 minutes til landfall. Bret set the basket down. It was a kid named Garret. He was probably ten or twelve with a stupid trendy haircut and a skateboard. He was crying. His face was bright red, smeared with tears and snot. Bret rolled his eyes and sighed heavily.

"Go home kid" he yelled out to the crying child as he ran over to Bret.

"My parents went to the store, and they aren't back yet and I don't know where they are and I'm scared and can I please come with you in your bunker I heard you had one I'm so scared,", he gushed in a torrent.

Just then Kevin appeared as well. He was carrying his stupid cat.

"Hey there neighbor. Do you mind if we bunker down with you for a bit? Just until whatever this is blows over. Me and Biscuits here won't take up much room," Keven implored.

"Go home both of you. I only have enough supplies for me. There's no room. And if you think I would let some useless cat come down there with me, you're crazy" he barked as he picked up the basket and headed into the bunker.

He kept his back to them, deliberately using his body and the basket to block the entrance as he went through. Bret could still hear the little boy sobbing. "Only the strong survive kiddo", Bret thought to himself. It really only now stuck him how many of his neighbors probably knew about his bunker. More might come and try to break in or take his supplies. As soon as he got through the entrance, he slammed the lock closed behind him. He could hear the faint sounds of the kid crying and the muffled voice of Kevin through the heavy door.

The space was decently large. The old canning cellar had been big, and Bret had converted the whole room into a bunker. There was a kitchen area with a sink, stove, refrigerator, and chest freezer. There was a living room set up with a sofa and television. A half-wall partition separated a small bedroom area and bathroom with toilet and shower. It was very much like a normal in-law unit except that the walls were lined with shelves and cupboards containing supplies. No sooner had he gotten down the short flight of stairs and set the basket on the floor, there was a boom. It reverberated through the house and the room went dark. Was that it? Was that the big one? Bret held his breath in the dark, waiting for the aftershock. He thought about his neighbors. The kid and Kevin and his cat standing outside.

He figured they were ash now or at least pulverized by the impact wave. He pictured all the smug yuppies dying of radiation while he sat safe and sound in the bunker. He couldn't help but to smile.

After a few minutes the backup power from the solar battery cells kicked on. Thinking about his neighbors getting flash fried by the nuclear strike, he walked over to one of the cupboards and took out a box of anti-radiation iodine pills. He swallowed a couple dry and sat down on the sofa. He looked at his phone. No reception down here. It figured. The whole situation seemed so unreal. It had happened. It had really happened.

After a while Bret got up and walked to one of the food shelves. He decided that he deserved something sweet to start off his new post-apocalyptic life and selected the case of Pop Tarts. When he picked it up it felt too light. He turned the box around and to his horror found that the package had been chewed open and something had eaten the majority of its contents. Nearly the entire case had been ruined. There were holes chewed in all the packaging and the contents had been replaced by little rodent droppings. He did finally find a single packet out of the entire case that had not yet been chewed. He took his prize and returned to the sofa. How had this happened? He had never had a mouse problem. How had it even gotten in the room? This room was supposed to be secure and sealed. If a mouse could get in did that mean that the radiation could too? With that thought he jumped up and got out the iodine pills again. This time taking two.

Bret went over to the little wall mounted screen that controlled the security system. He wanted to check the exterior cameras and see what was going on outside. It was showing several error messages. He scrolled through the various camera feeds. All five exterior cameras and seven interior ones were showing an "offline "error message. Could they have been damaged in the explosion? Did an EMP wipe them out? He didn't think the house was damaged. He hadn't heard or felt anything fall. He could understand the external cameras getting knocked around in the impact wave, but the interior ones should be fine. The motion sensors were not responding either. Couldn't be an EMP because the display screen was working. His phone was still working even if he had no reception down in the bunker. He did notice that the Wi-Fi was down. His phone might be totally useless without it but the security system was hard wired. He knew how finicky Wi-Fi and Bluetooth could be and figured a wired system would hold up better. It seemed however, that there must be an issue with the wiring. He needed to see what was going on outside and couldn't risk popping his head out into the poisoned radioactive air out there. The expensive, complex air filtration system that he had had installed would keep him safe as long as he stayed inside. He wouldn't risk exposure outside, but he needed to see what was happening.

He had installed the security system himself and knew where the wires ran. He had even put in a handy panel in the wall for easy access to the connection hub that the wires from all the cameras and sensors connected to as well as the Wi-Fi router. That way he could more easily add additional devices as he wanted. He opened the access panel and his breath caught in his throat. What had been a neat and orderly figuration of wires was now tangled and cut to pieces. This definitely explained why the system was down. Had someone come down here and sabotaged him? Who would do such a thing? Why? Probably some jealous asshole. As he looked closer though he saw that the wires had not been cut. Rather, they had been chewed. Then he noticed the droppings. A mouse! A mouse had done this! That little bastard had completely destroyed his security system and router. It hit Bret then that he was totally alone. He had no way of seeing outside or making contact with anyone. He was only an hour into the apocalypse, and he was already fucked. He needed to sit down. Flopping down on the couch he tried to take some deep breaths and calm down. At least there was still power.

His mind went back to the damaged case of Pop Tarts. Bret jumped up and went over to one of the food storage shelves. Almost every box he inspected had been chewed open and the contents half eaten and covered in rodent droppings. Over the next few hours, he inspected every box and individual package of food. The pile of uncontaminated food was depressingly small. What had been a year or more worth of food was now only a few weeks. Thank goodness for the canned goods. No one was going to chew through that! There was enough to feed him for a while at least. Hopefully they would last long enough for him to figure out what to do next.

The day had been exhausting. Bret took the "Saving Private Ryan" DVD off a shelf and popped it in the player. Settling in on the sofa to watch his favorite movie would soothe his nerves. Within a few minutes he was asleep.

When Bret woke up the movie was over, and the menu screen was on the television. He glanced at his watch. It was 10pm. He could hear something. It was faint but it was there. It was a scratching sound. He could hear it in the wall. Rubbing the sleep from his eyes Bret tried to focus on the sound and triangulate its origin. The sound was coming from the other side of the room. With horror he realized it was coming from the air vent. The air filtration and recirculation system were possibly the most important feature of his bunker. He couldn't allow that to become contaminated with mouse droppings.

Using a little step ladder, he climbed up and removed the vent to peek inside. His fear was confirmed. There was definitely a nest in the vent. As he looked at it though he made a second terrible observation. The nesting material appeared to be made of shredded pieces of the air filter system. Did this mean that he wasn't getting filtered air? Was the fan just pumping radiation into the bunker? He ran over to the bed and grabbed the blankets off of it. Frantically he shoved them into the vent, blocking it as best as he could. He replaced the vent cover and sealed it with duct tape as best as he could. It wasn't perfect but it would hopefully be enough. Was he already feeling dizzy? Is that why he had felt so tired earlier? In a panic he grabbed a box of anti-radiation iodine pills. He hurriedly popped several out of the blister pack and swallowed them down. Again, he went to the sofa for a quick rest. Rest and clarity were needed if he was going to survive.

For all the preparations that Bret had made it seemed that the universe had found his blind spot. He had been ready for civil unrest, fire, flood, and even nuclear war but it seemed he was no match for one of God's tiniest, most unassuming creatures. The desire to crush its tiny little head was strong. He always hated vermin but now it went so much deeper. These little fuckers had to be destroyed. Of course, there wasn't any poison in the bunker though. He would have to handle it the old-fashioned way. Closing his eyes, he imagined his bloody victory over the tiny foe.

After his nap Bret got his 9mm out of the laundry basket. Smiling to himself, he started loading it. A sudden wave of dizziness forced him to slump down onto the floor. The radiation must be taking its toll he thought. How long had it been since the bomb fell? Maybe two days? Time was getting funny. He felt so tired. With his head swimming he pulled himself up and staggered over to his iodine pills. This time he emptied an entire blister pack. Fighting down his gorge he chewed the pills and swallowed them. Maybe he should eat something? No, the cans are probably contaminated by the radiation. That's most likely why his stomach is so upset. It was starting to really hurt.

Fighting back the dizziness, pain and nausea, he set his jaw and strained his ears to listen for the sounds of the enemy. He pressed his ear against the wall and gripped the pistol with a hand gone clammy. He waited what felt like an eternity. Then he heard something. Not from the wall but over by the food shelf. Yes! There! There was movement on the bottom shelf near a ruined box of ramen. Spinning around to face the tiny intruder he let several shots fly. Did he get it? Walking over, he saw no tiny corpse. A sound came from the bedroom area. He stomped and wobbled his way over to the source of the sound. In the corner! There it was! He shot again. Missed. Damnit! He had the little bastard on the run now. As it ran along the base of the concrete wall Bret shot wildly. The bullets gouged chunks out of the cinder block and the sound in that enclosed space was deafening. He unloaded his extended magazine with abandon. Finally, a shot landed. There was a small explosion of red that splashed up the wall. When he started to walk towards what was left of his tiny foe, he realized something was wrong.

Looking down he saw that blood was pouring down his leg from a wound in his lower stomach. A ricochet had hit him. What was he thinking? How did this happen?

Bret staggered to the sofa. He could feel the life draining out of him. Laying down he grabbed a throw pillow and used it to apply pressure to the wound. That stupid mouse was going to kill him. That tiny little shit had taken him out. Rage filled him. All the work he had put it meant nothing. He would have survived if it hadn't been for that stupid mouse.

Just then there was a banging at the door. A voice came faintly from the other side, but he couldn't make out what it was saying through the thick metal. He started to sit up but quickly found it too difficult. Instead, he yelled from where he lay.

"Fuck off! Find your own shelter. I don't have anything for you. If you don't leave, I'm gonna come out there and make you," Bret barked.

Every word was a lightning bolt of pain. He strained to listen from his spot on the couch. The faint voice kept on talking and Bret could hear the muffled sound of a fist pounding on the reinforced steel door. Bret's head was swimming. The sounds from outside seemed distant and disconnected.

"Did I fucking stutter? Get off my property before I come out there and make you! You're on your own bud," Bret responded.

Bret listened but got no response. Who was that and who did they think they were coming here. Did they want to beg for shelter? Steal his supplies? It wasn't his fault that his neighbors weren't as prepared as he was. Besides, he had enough to deal with without also taking care of someone else. He kept the pressure on his wound. It would be fine. Once the bleeding stopped, he would stitch himself up. It would be fine. He needed to rest up incase more "neighbors "came to loot his supplies. He just needed a nap and he'd be fine. His eyes drifted closed. His mind relaxed into a dark twilight. Never had he felt exhaustion like this. He gave in to it. He was unsure how long he laid there before he was distantly aware of tiny feet scampering across him. He managed to pry his eyes open slightly. Sitting on his chest and staring back at him was a little grey mouse. As Bret looked into those shining black eyes, he thought he could understand why people found these things so cute. Its little whiskers twitched as it sniffed his chin with a tiny pink nose. Then Bret closed his eyes for the last time and succumbed to the lasting night of death. The stray bullet had nicked a vital organ and slowly he had bled out.

***

Kevin led the firemen and EMTs around the back of the house to the bunker door.

"It's been over a week since I've been able to get him to talk to me. I thought I heard gunshots from outside. I was surprised he was still down there but he's kind of weird so maybe I shouldn't have been. I came over to see if he was ok. I told him that it was ok to come out. That everything was fine, but he just got angry. He was pretty pissy. He threatened to shoot me, so I just left. I went back yesterday but he didn't answer my knocking. Figured he was mad or something. The neighborhood has been a little worried about him. Pretty sure he's been down there since that fake emergency alert thing," he told a fireman.

"I heard they caught the guy that hacked the system. Some teenager messing around on his computer. He called it a prank. I hope they fry his ass. People went nuts. Two people died in that car that hit the power station down the street. People panicked so much. It was chaos," the firemen said back.

"I remember that. The explosion was so loud. I could hear it from across town at my house. Hopefully the repairs will be done soon," an EMT said.

The firemen banged at the door and yelled for Bret to open it. No response. After giving it a few whacks with his ax he called for someone to bring a saw and the jaws of life. As they pried the door open bit by bit, the smell of death began to waft out. By the time they got down into the room the dead body on the couch was no surprise. It was easy to see the wound in his stomach and the blood that soaked through the sofa and pooled on the floor. Bret still had the gun in his hand. They spotted the exploded mouse carcass along with the pockmarks in the walls and it didn't take long for them to piece together what happened. The other EMT picked up one of the empty blister packs from the iodine pills.

"Oh shit. If he actually ate all of these then he would have been in big trouble even without that wound. People think this stuff is harmless but it's toxic as hell in large doses. Terrible way to go. Causes psychosis too. Why does no one read the warning labels?" he said, shaking his head.

"Looks like the rodents had their way with him too" the EMT said, examining the torn and missing flesh on Bret's face. He noticed movement under the dead man's shirt. Lifting the hem of the gore-soaked t-shirt revealed a gaping hole in the abdomen of the dead man. In the hollow where the corpse's organs should be there were bits of cloth and sofa stuffing. It was a nest. Nestled in it was a tiny grey mouse cuddling several pink squirming babies. The scene was oddly sweet and despite himself the EMT smiled.

TOBY AND ROSCO

The new house was big. It had a big front porch and a big backyard with a big old oak tree in it. The kitchen was big too. Toby's mom had said it was the kind of kitchen that makes you want to bake pies. Toby's new room was also big. Bigger than his old room. Even his humongous new bed seemed small in the giant room. It was a special bed with knobs and gadgets that made it go up and down and the wheels that let them move it. There was a picture window that took up much of one wall. Sometimes Toby's parents would wheel his bed to the window so that he could look out at the stately oak tree that sat in the middle of the expansive grassy yard. He wanted nothing more than to run through that grass. For now, though, the little boy would have to settle for feeling the sun's warmth through the window glass.

Machines took up much of the space in the big new room. Toby's world the beeping machines and the tubes and wires that ran from them. He missed his old house. He missed running down the hall to hug his mom when she got home from work. He missed playing in the small yard with his friends. He missed having friends. He missed when his mom and dad smiled for real. Sure, they tried their best to put on a happy face around him, but Toby could see the sadness in their eyes.

In his heart he did understand that what he missed was his old life. He knew that they had needed to move to be closer to the special doctor that his parents said he needed. He knew that he might never be able to run in the yard again. He knew he would never get to go back to school or play tag with his friends.

Toby looked over at the card that his teacher, Mrs. Brenton brought him last week. The entire second grade had signed it. His friend Jessica drew a heart in it for him. She had never visited though. None of them had. In a way, Toby was ok with that. He didn't want to make them sad. He didn't want to see any more forced smiles and sad, pitying eyes. The way people looked at him now made Toby uncomfortable. They saw him there all tiny and skinny and bald and it made them sad. They didn't want to be around him. Even his dad. He could see how upset his dad got every time he looked at him.

Toby thought about how he and his dad used to play catch and go fishing. He was so proud of Toby when he threw the ball really far or baited his own hook. He'd call Toby "champ" and tell him what a good job he did. Now Toby could barely stand up by himself. Recently he had even started wetting the bed again like a baby. He knew it was the sickness, but he just wanted his dad to be proud of him again. Toby wanted his dad to sit with him without looking like he couldn't wait to get away. Mom was different though. She was the only one that treated him normal. Well, sort of. She still had that sadness in her eyes, but she didn't look away or try to hide it. Sometimes she would just hug him and not let go until toby said "ok mom. That's enough. You're going to squish me!". There were some nights that she would get home from work and just climb in the big bed with Toby, and he would fall asleep in her arms like when he was little. Those nights were good ones.

Nighttime was bad in the big new house. The shadow of the tree outside crawled in through the window and stretched up his walls. The high ceilings made for deep inky corners where anything could hide. Many nights Toby found it hard to sleep while he imagined all the ghouls that could be watching him from those shadows.

***

After a few weeks had gone by Toby learned to live with the creepy shadows that grew in the night. He knew that big boys weren't afraid of the dark. Plus, his dad had gotten him a nightlight shaped like the hammer his favorite superhero used to smash bad guys. That made Toby feel a lot better.

Just as he was getting used to the room though, that's when the scratching began. It started in the closet and sounded like huge claws scraping at the door from inside. Something was in there and it wanted out. It wanted him. That night Toby had screamed, and both his parents came running. In tears he told them there was a monster that was trying to get him, and it was in the closet. They opened the closed door to reveal nothing but winter coats and toys that he no longer played with. His parents tucked him back in with reassurances that it must be squirrels in the attic. Toby could see the logic in that, but it had sounded so much bigger and, in his closet, and *not* the attic.

Things were quiet for a few nights after that, but then it came again. This time it was even more vicious. He could hear claws madly scraping at the other side of his closet door. In the dim light he could see the closet door shaking with the force of the monster trying to get out. Toby screamed as loud as his sick little body would let him. His parents came dashing through the door, eyes wild with their own fear. They expected an emergency of a medical nature. The tension visibly left their shoulders as they followed Toby's shaking finger to the closet door. It was easy to forget that the normal tasks of parenthood still had to be performed. Sick children still needed their closets checked for monsters. His mother's face softened as she came over to the bed to comfort her terrified child. Toby's father went to the closet to check it. Through hitching sobs and wheezing breaths, the boy tried to explain the sounds and how he really *really* had heard them.

His father turned on the closet light and instructed him to look for himself. Toby strained his eyes to study the contents of the closet as best as he could from his position in the bed. His father pointed to the inside of the door and the lack of any scratches or blemishes on the painted wood. The door looked brand new. Toby was so confused. He *KNEW* that he had heard it. The door had been rattling in its frame!

His mother stroked his head and explained that sometimes the medicines that are so helpful and keep him alive can also do things that aren't so helpful, like make him think there is something in the closet. It was normal she said, and he just had to remember that it was the medicine doing it and it wasn't real. She promised to talk to his doctor about it at the next appointment and kissed him on the forehead. His father suggested that they leave the closet door open and the light inside of it on. Monsters hate light after all so it would keep them from coming back. Toby agreed and his parents tucked him back in. They both had worry in their eyes, but Toby somehow knew it was not the monster that bothered them.

Toby stayed awake staring into his closet. Studying the contents from the confines of the bed, he no longer felt fear, but a profound sadness. There was no monster, but the space was filled top to bottom with the ghosts of his old life. There was a snowsuit hanging next to a pirate Halloween costume. His baseball bat and glove sat to one side. Toby wondered if he would ever be able to use these things again. People talked often about how great it will be when he gets better. How he's a little fighter and he can beat this. His parents used to say things like that but hadn't in a while. Toby's doctors never said things like that. They had all stopped talking about the future at some point.

Just as the child's mind was on the edge of an understanding that no child should ever have to grapple with-- his old baseball came rolling out of the closet. In the dead silence of the house, the sound it made rolling on the wood floor was deafening. A whimper escaped his lips, and he clutched the blanket, pulling it over his head. The inherent instinct of a child to hide from danger kicked in; that magical belief that every child instinctively has that a blanket is all the protection one's needs against monsters.

He strained his ears for any further horrors. He could hear the scratching. It was softer, like claws tapping on the wall. It sounded like talons sliding slowly on wood. Toby's mind painted a picture of a great hairy, hulking beast with long thin fingers tipped with sharp, shining claws. He imagined a demon with glowing green eyes peeling through the back of his closet, before pulling itself forward into the room. He heard the claws clacking on the floor as it crept towards him. Toby's bladder let go. He shivered in terror. Tears soaked the blanket held tightly over his face. Distantly he heard the beeping of his heart monitor increasing. He didn't need the machine to tell him that his heart was pounding hard enough to break free of his little chest. The scraping, clicking claws were getting closer.

Time had slowed to a painful trickle. Every second was an eon of terror. Suddenly something took hold of the blanket, tearing it from the boy. Toby wasn't aware that he was screaming until his parents burst into the room. They found him, their frail little child in his urine-soaked pajamas, face contorted in fear-- exposed and terrified in the middle of the overly large hospital bed. They ran to him. His mother held him while his father collected the soiled linens and fetched clean pajamas. Toby tried through his tears and wheezing breaths to explain the horrific ghoul that was trying to get him. They made soothing noises and petted his head. They didn't believe him. They didn't understand.

***

At Toby's next doctors visit his parents described the "night terrors" he had been experiencing. They asked the doctor if it was maybe a side effect of the medication. The adults all agreed that he needed a sedative to help him sleep. None of them asked Toby.

The sedatives helped Toby sleep, but they did nothing to stop the nightly visitations from the closet ghoul. Night after night he heard the scraping, scratching claws. Toby squeezed his eyes shut and hid under his blankets. He did his best to stay silent though. His parents didn't believe him and therefore could not help him. He bore his terror in silence and solitude. This was now just another facet of his lonely little life. He was sick and small, terrified…and utterly alone.

The monster became bolder with each night. It pulled at Toby's blanket while cowered beneath it. It clacked and scraped across the room to stand over him. Toby kept his head covered and his eyes squeezed tightly shut, but in his mind, he could clearly see the great beast looming above him, fetid slime dripping from its toothy maw. Toby could hear it breathing. The monster panted into Toby's ear. Every night the ghoul crept from the closet to torment the frail little child. The loneliness that had accompanied his illness deepened further with the appearance of the apparition. Simply put, no one believed him. All the adults dismissed it as a side effect of his meds. They all thought he was just crazy now on top of being sick. It just made that sad piteous look in their eyes deepen.

Time passed and Toby got weaker and weaker. His life was all tubes and wires now. Tubes fed him. Tubes in his nose helped him breathe. He even had tubes to help him use the bathroom. Aunts and uncles and cousins and family he hadn't seen since he was tiny, came into his room to visit and squeeze his tiny hand and give him smiles that didn't reach their eyes. Toby just stared out the window or straight up at the ceiling. No one talked about the future or what a little "fighter" he is. Mom and Dad had almost stopped talking, like they didn't know what to say. The thing that Toby's mind was struggling previously to understand was now abundantly clear to him. He was dying. He wasn't going to get better. He was never going back to school. He was never going to learn how to throw a fast ball. He was never going to do anything. He would just waste away. Getting smaller and smaller in his giant bed in his giant room. Smaller and weaker, until one day there would be nothing left.

The closet monster kept coming every night. Sometimes Toby felt too weak to pull the blankets up, and instead just shut his eyes against the creature. He felt the bounce, and shift of pressure on his bed as the thing climbed up and sat. Every night now it would just sit at the foot of Toby's bed, probably staring at him with those glowing demon eyes. It was probably waiting

for him to sleep so it could eat him, the boy thought. He wasn't
sure if he cared. Toby was so tired.

◊

Rosco wanted nothing more than to be a good boy. It was
hard though. He missed his mom. He did not remember her
very well, but she had been warm and soft, and he had felt safe
with her and his litter mates. That seemed like so long ago now.
No matter what he did now, it seemed he was being bad. All
Rosco wanted to do was play. At least no one hit him now
though, not like his old humans. He knew that they were bad,
but he still missed them. They cuddled him and gave him pats
sometimes, especially at first. Rosco missed cuddles and pats.

The lady had been nice. She would kiss Rosko's face and
give him a bite of whatever she was eating. The man had not
been nice at all. He played mean tricks on Rosco. The man
would hold out a piece of food but if Rosco tried to take it, the
man would smack his nose, *hard*. The man smacked him a lot.
Any time Rosco went wee, the man hit him. He couldn't

understand why. Outside would have been his preference, but the humans never let him. He would have much rather gone out for his business and maybe chased some of those squirrels that ran around the big tree in the yard. They just never seemed to remember to let him out. Rosco tried to tell them he wanted out, but the man just yelled. He tried so hard to be good, but he could only hold it for so long and eventually would always make a mess.

When he started growing big, the lady must not have thought he was very cute anymore. She stopped giving him kisses and bites of food. She started yelling and smacking him like the man did. Rosco was too big now to be on the sofa or the bed. When he tried to cuddle her like before, she just yelled and shewed him away.

The humans were also so forgetful. That could make it very hard to be good. When they forgot to fill his bowl, Rosco would get hungry. He knew that stealing his humans' food was bad boy behavior, but he would get so hungry that he couldn't think right. The man hit him hard when that happened. Then came the closet…

The humans started putting Rosco in the closet in the spare bedroom when he was being bad. It was dark and scary in there. He cried and clawed at the door. He panicked and howled. Eventually the woman would always let him out. After a while though, she didn't. One of the humans would throw his bowl in the closet with him and leave him there. He cried and barked. The space was so small that he had to lay in his own mess. Rosco hated it. He was so hungry and thirsty all the time. Sores started to form from the filth, and he hurt all over. Too tired to bark, the humans seemed to forget about him.

He wasn't sure when or how it happened but suddenly Rosko didn't hurt anymore. He couldn't smell the stink around him. Looking down, he saw himself curled up on the floor of the closet.

***

Time passed very strangely after that. Rosco figured out how to push himself through the closet door move through the house. It was empty now. His humans were gone. When had they gone? He missed them. Rosco did his best to stay away from the guest room and the closet but sometimes he just found himself back in there again. A panic would overtake him, and he would scratch furiously at the door until after a time he would remember that he could simply walk through it.

No one was there to yell or hit Rosco anymore. He did not feel hungry or thirsty or cold. No one was there though. Just him. It was so lonely. He often found himself back in the closet, crying. The little dog knew that he was not really supposed to be there but could not for the life of him figure out where to go or what to do.

Many times, he tried going outside. It seemed logical enough that he could go through the back door and into the yard the same way he could pass through the closet door when he tried hard enough. It was no use though. The back door was solid for him. Rosco stared longingly at the big yard with the tree full of squirrels. He imagined what the grass would feel like under his paws. Then he would get sad again and find himself back in the closet.

Then the boy arrived! Rosco was overjoyed. He barked and jumped with excitement. Quickly it was clear that the boy could not see him. At first that really upset Rosco, and he would find himself back in the closet, sad and scared. Nothing would stop him from continuing to try, however. He found the boys toy ball and tried to push it. It took some time, but he persisted until he was able to roll the ball across the floor to the boy. The boy screamed. Maybe he was afraid of dogs?

Rosco kept trying to show the boy that he was a good boy and just wanted to play. He pulled the boy's covers and jumped on the bed. The little dog began to realize that the frail little boy might never stop being scared of him. The bed shook with his trembling and quiet weeping. Rosco felt awful. He knew that feeling. He recognized that look in the boy's eyes. Rosco knew exactly what that fear felt like. He was so ashamed. All he wanted was to play. When the boy moved in Rosco had been so excited that he hadn't considered the possibility of the boy not wanting to be his friend. Eventually Rosco just lay on the bed and cried quietly along with the boy. They could at least be alone together.

◊

It was very late, and Toby was still laying with the blanket pulled over his head, waiting for sleep to come. As always, the monster was sitting at the foot of his bed. It was becoming a routine. Suddenly the machines and monitors surrounding his bed started beeping and wailing. Startled, Toby popped his head out of the blankets to see what was happening. When he did, the sight that greeted him was not what he had expected at all…

The sun was up and shining through the window in golden beams. Hadn't it been night only a moment ago? Toby supposed sleep did come swiftly like that sometimes and the medication often made him lose time or feel confused. This felt different though. The noisy machines sounded far away. Then Toby noticed the dog. On the foot of the bed, staring at him with bright excited eyes and wide puppy smile was a little white pit bull. He had always wanted a dog, but his parents said he wasn't old enough and once he got sick it was out of the question. Toby sat up and put a hand towards the dog. He knew you were supposed to let them sniff your hand first. Not waiting to stand on ceremony, the dog spang up onto Toby's lap and knocked him back with enthusiastic kisses.

The dog jumped down from the bed and scurried over to the closet. When it bounded back it had Toby's baseball in its mouth. It looked at him imploringly and wiggled with enthusiasm. It glanced out the window at the beautiful golden day then back again at Toby. Without thinking, Toby sprang from the bed.

"You want to go outside buddy?" he asked, grinning ear to ear.

In his excitement, Toby did not think to question his sudden energy or lack of pain. He had not spared a glance for the sick, broken shell that he left behind him in the bed. The boy just stampeded through the house with his new best friend-- caught in this moment of joy. They got to the back door and Toby flung it open wide. The sunlit yard stretched out before them into a grassy meadow. The air was so fresh and clean like a spring afternoon. They ran into the light, feeling the soft grass beneath their feet. They ran free from pain or fear. Neither would ever be alone or lonely again.

A NOTE HOME

Dear Mrs. Shleige,

I want to start off by saying that I really enjoy having Kaleb in my class. He's one of the brightest third graders I've ever had. His reading comprehension is fantastic, and his math is simply off the charts. He's even taken to making up his own nonsense equations for fun. When I try to look at them, sometimes I get a headache, and there was that one time it made my nose bleed, but it's so wonderful to see him be that enthusiastic.

We have talked before about the issues he's been having socializing, but he seems to have overcome that quite nicely. Being new can be difficult. Children can have a tough time adapting to new social situations, but Kaleb is flourishing. The other children seem to like him, and he never lacks for playmates or company at lunch time. Really a delightful young man, and we all agree.

Last week on Valentine's Day when he came in with those cute little clay figures he made for everyone, it was a big hit. Many of my students still carry the figurines with them in their pockets or keep them on their desks. Normally I wouldn't allow it, but I like looking at them, as well. In fact, the one he gave me is sitting on my desk now.

All of that isn't why I wanted to reach out to you, though. Today there was an incident with a therapy dog that visited our class. They are supposed to have great training and be calm, but as soon as it came into our classroom, the dog started barking and growling. It pulled away from its handler and lunged at poor Kaleb. Thank goodness it didn't hurt him badly—just a little scratch before the dog was subdued. It was so terrifying for the other children. Several of them were crying.

We love Kaleb so much. We would never let any harm come to him. But not to worry: the other students and I took care of that vicious beast—and its handler, as well, for allowing such aggression toward our Kaleb. I'll be keeping their heads here in my class for a while if you would like to see. Kaleb thanked the class and told us all what a good job we did. I hope it's okay. I hope we did good. We would do anything for him.

Kindest of regards,

Mrs. Simon

<u>EYEWITNESS</u>

"Well, it happened almost four years ago" she began. "I hadn't told anyone else until I posted about it on that forum online. I didn't want anyone to think I was crazy but that seemed like an ok place to share. Then you messaged me and here we are."

"Yes, thank you for responding to my request and thank you for agreeing to meet with me," the man in the suit said, tapping the pen he was holding against the spiral binding of his notebook. The woman sitting on her sofa nervously smoothed her skirt then went on

"I was living in a small town in northern California. My work was super close to home so I would go home on my lunch break to walk my dog and have lunch with him. On this particular day I popped home around 2pm or so and it was a bright, pleasant day. The sun was shining. It was beautiful out. My property was very private and surrounded by tall trees and pedestrian traffic on my road wasn't really a thing. I walked out into the back yard with my dog when a tall, older looking, very pale white man with light hair and a black suit appeared about 20 feet away from where I was standing in my yard. I didn't turn a corner and see him, and it wasn't from the corner of my eye. He just appeared. Like, just THERE." She paused and took a deep breath. "I looked fully at him in the mid-afternoon sun. He was there. He was there just long enough for me to fully see him. We made eye contact -- maybe about three or four seconds -- then he was gone. He didn't blink out or walk away. One moment he existed and the next he simply did not." She looked at the interviewer sitting across from her. She couldn't read his face, couldn't tell if the stern man with his reasonable brown leather shoes believed her. "I had the thought that 'well I guess I'm crazy now' and went about my business."

"You went back to work?" the man asked.

"Yeah, I did. I just kind of tried to forget it. I didn't know what to do with it, about it. What could I have done?".

"You didn't tell anyone?".

"No. Who would I tell? Who would believe it? People would just assume I was losing it."

"Were you? I mean, is it possible you hallucinated it? Have you ever had a hallucination or vivid daydream like that before?" he asked as he continued to scribble notes on his pad.

"I've done acid and stuff when I was younger. I know what a hallucination is like. This was real. He was real. For a while I thought maybe he was a ghost or something. Until the fire anyway."

"Yes, tell me about the fire," he leaned in a bit. She took another deep steadying breath. It was obvious that she was getting a bit uncomfortable. It was still raw.

"Well, the fire was about a month later, in November. Well, it was Paradise, where I lived, and my house was on Pentz Rd. near lower Pearson. It was one of the worst hit neighborhoods with a high casualty rate. We got trapped in our car trying to escape and had to abandon it and run on foot. There was a wall of fire. Several of the people in cars around me didn't survive. I'm sure you probably heard about it. There were a couple documentaries." The interviewer nodded solemnly. "I've heard of Men in Black showing up before and after disasters so maybe that's what it was. It was an interesting experience for sure."

"Has anyone else contacted you to speak about your experience?" the man asked.

"No, just you."

"Good, good," he responded. "I'll just need you to sign a couple forms and I'll be on my way. I'm going to have to ask you not tell anyone else about this though."

He took some papers from the briefcase beside his chair. He carried the papers over to her on the sofa and sat next to her, handing her his pen.

"Who did you say you were with? Homeland?" she asked as she took the papers and began to look over them. By the time she registered the prick of the syringe in her neck she was already going limp and fading to black.

The man took a phone from his pocket and made a call.

"Yes, it's been taken care of. I think we were able to get ahead of this one. Go ahead and send the clean-up team."

THE AUTHOR

Miss Rabbit is an interdimensional Bog Witch that lives in the deep dark woods with her partner and a menagerie of beasts.

You can find her other titles, audiobooks, art, and more at www.JackieRabbit.com